T0064587

Stephanie's Stepside, Episode 2:

Blood on Toxic Ground

by
Lonnie Mair

authorHOUSE®

AuthorHouse™
1663 Liberty Drive
Bloomington, IN 47403
www.authorhouse.com
Phone: 1 (800) 839-8640

Published by AuthorHouse   05/11/2015

ISBN: 978-1-5049-0810-8 (sc)
ISBN: 978-1-5049-0823-8 (e)

Library of Congress Control Number: 2015906187

Print information available on the last page.

Any people depicted in stock imagery provided by Thinkstock are models, and such images are being used for illustrative purposes only. Certain stock imagery © Thinkstock.

This book is printed on acid-free paper.

Contents

Acknowledgement

As was the case in *Stephanie's Stepside,* much of the reason a reader might experience pleasurable reading in this sequel, is due to the editing skills of Carol Mair, a multitalented woman, whom I am fortunate to be able to call my wife. It was she who untangled the grammatical Gordian knot that my writing became while I was in search of the most descriptively accurate and picturesque phrases to carry the developing plot, characters, setting, and symbolism of this effort. However, *Stephanie's Stepside* and this sequel are mine, and what errors which may have slipped through the proofreading process, are no fault of hers, but rather are those of this writer who too often knew what he wanted to say, but failed to realize that, although the grammatical constructions may have been in his head, they weren't on the paper.

Author/Illustrator's comment on the cover illustration

The author does not pretend to be an accomplished artist, but as he did for the cover of his first book, *Stephanie's Stepside,* he has illustrated the cover for his second book: *Stephanie Stepside Episode 2: Blood on Toxic Ground.* His purpose was to give the reader an idea of the physical setting of much of the story.

Author's comment in reference to weapons mentioned

In this work there are some references to weapons. The author occasionally used artistic license, for example in the components of a certain bomb. However, the specific information on the weapons made reference to in this work, the author found freely available on the internet.

Author's comment in reference to the term "stepside"

The term stepside, in connection with a pickup truck, is a description of a particular construction of the bed of the pickup. A stepside pickup has the walls of the pickup bed inside the wheel wells of the truck's bed. This construction allows for an exterior step forward of the rear wheels, yet behind the cab. This exterior step is meant to provide easy access to the contents of the truck's bed from the side of the pickup, in addition to the access provided by the truck's tailgate. Another advantage of this type of pickup bed construction is that the interior of the pickup bed is not restricted by the presence of the wheel wells, creating a completely rectangular storage volume of the space of the pickup bed. The Chevrolet stepside pickup has a long history, first appearing in 1924.

Disclaimer

This story is a work of fiction, and, although places and names may be recognizable, any resemblance to people, living or dead, is not intentional, but rather, purely coincidental.

Although there are companies that operate similar-in-function business operations in the Central Valley, this work is not an accusation of them, their business practices, or their personnel, nor should it be construed to be.

The universities are real, the people and conditions are total fiction. I am not associated with the universities in any way, and, although I do not think there are any negative aspersions that can legitimately be viewed as cast in this work, it was not my intention to do so.

The Central Valley does contain the geologic realities and potentialities referred to in this work, and, should an earthquake of the magnitude mentioned occur, there is no doubt that the damage would be extensive. To what extent and to what degree the damage would be, I leave to other minds to calculate.

Dedication to Lora Mair

It is with a great deal of pleasure that I dedicate this, my second book, to my mother, Lora Mair. It was she who first had the dubious honor of reading my prose, with the purpose of sifting it, to make sure it did what it was supposed to do. More than once, the sifting of prose was juxtaposed with the sifting of flour during food preparation, since that was the time she had. Hers was a discerning eye, quite probably wishing I was more productive in my use of time.

It is quite possible that the strong work ethic that permeated my mother's life came from the large rural farming family in which she was born and raised, just one valley over from the famed Lora Ingalls Wilder of Wisconsin, during the days of the Great Depression. A succession of strong matriarchs in her own family preceded my mother.

The love that she had for her family, and theirs' for her, was so mutually evident by their interactions that there were no misunderstandings in that regard. That understanding translated well into the family which she raised, three rambunctious boys with enough energy to drive any working mother frazzled on some nights, I would imagine. A husband whose work him kept him pretty well occupied during the week, combined with church work on the weekends, kept him busy much of that time as well. For quite a while, my mother also augmented my father's church work and filled the role of a church pastor's wife, in addition to her other roles of second wage earner, homemaker, mother, homework checker, and listening ear for all issues that young boys were not yet ready to share with their father.

The willingness to help with the family's resources continued, when she and Dad opened a donut house in Lemoore, California after Dad's first retirement from teaching, a business that suffered due to its very success! The principles simply weren't young enough anymore to be able to devote sufficient energy over the long haul to continue to keep up with the demand that they had created. Later, a school secretary, a real estate agent, a notary public and self -employed with a business providing office services, to name only a few, were jobs with which she finished her working career.

I am happy to report that at this writing, my mother is still sharp of mind and an avid reader, crossword solver, as well as a jigsaw puzzler, and continues to be the core center of care and love around which the family revolves and maintains its cohesion and equilibrium and it my hope that she will be able to read this dedication when the book comes out in print!

Chapter One

Sniper Attack!

The gray-black asphalt road stretched west toward a ridge of low hills, dominated by three more predominate larger hills, whose shapes were distorted by the heat waves that wavered over the fields, like gently undulating opaque blankets. In the more immediate distance, a shape coalesced from the heat as it neared the road. The sweat stained brim of a hat topped an outfit that was neither brand new nor past it's prime. The jeans had that comfortable look, the stiffness gone, yet not full of holes that once had been a style worn by those who had never seen the kind of work that would have produced the worn out look in the first place. A proportioned denim shirt, filled comfortably in the right places, testified that this was a woman who knew how she looked in the outfit, but didn't make a big deal about it. Beyond her, in the distance, was another shape, a now and then almost disappearing apparition, like unto the quivering heat radiating from the ground. The now evidently young woman approached an old, but well kept, red, stepside pickup truck, lowered the tailgate, and put onto the truck bed some soil test probes that she had produced from a well-worn field bag and put them into boxes that had been designed for them. Carefully closing the tailgate, she dusted herself off in a practiced motion and, opening the driver side door, reached inside the cab and behind the seat for a rag to wipe her boots before climbing into the cab. As she squatted to clean the gray, lifeless, dusty soil from them, she felt the brush of something against her hat and immediately heard the unmistakable report of a high-powered rifle. The bullet hit the solid curved steel of the old pickup with a heavy, solid, "spang," and caromed off into the lifeless heatwaves that undulated over the gray brown dustiness of flat, lifeless fields that stretched to the horizon. Moments later, the shape that had seemingly disappeared into the ground in the distant field resolved itself once again, and came around the front of the pickup. A quizzical look on the face of the so recent apparition turned into real concern, as it was this new arrival who realized that the new stain on the shirt and on the ground at her boots, had come from the oozing bright red flow from beneath the hat.

"Stephanie, sit down, you're bleeding!"

"Rachel, what are you doing here? I just left you taking sub-soil readings."

"Stephanie, I heard a shot! You've been hit!"

"Rachel, what on earth are you talking about?"

"Stephanie, come around to the other side of the truck, now!"

"Ok, ok, now, what is it you're so concerned about?"

"Stephanie, take off your hat and look at it," Rachel ordered.

As Stephanie did so, the realization of what had just happened hit her and she sagged onto the stepside of the old, red, Chevy pickup.

"I guess those guys are getting serious again," Stephanie whispered.

"Ya' think!" Rachel's eyes widened. "Wait a minute! You said, 'again.' This has happened before?"

"Oh, just that time at the university. They missed me and hit Professor Lackland," Stephanie replied.

That last answer startled Rachel, and she ducked behind the pickup.

"No use being a target," she said sheepishly, a bit embarrassed by her actions.

"That's one of the reasons I chose you for this job. You've got a head on your shoulders," Stephanie grinned and involuntarily winced at the motion.

Despite her instinctive action, Rachel produced a handkerchief and applied it to Stephanie's head, with the effect of stopping Stephanie's bleeding.

"What do you say we get out of here?" Rachel asked, and motioned for the keys. Stephanie gave no resistance and entered the passenger side of the pickup. The old, but well maintained engine roared to life and the pickup left a rising cloud of dust hanging in the heat filled air. Rachel was an expert driver and, although careful with the transmission, it was only seconds from the time she shifted into gear until she was going as fast as she thought the seasoned pickup could bear.

Rachel couldn't help remembering the first time she had begun to drive a standard shift pickup with her father at her side, wincing at the noises coming from the protesting transmission. "Thanks Dad, your patience paid off!" she murmured under her breath.

Chapter Two

Stepside Safety

Once inside the haven of the old stepside pickup that her father had so lovingly restored and customized for her, Stephanie had to admit to herself that the recent episode had shaken her up a bit. With a wry, inner grin she said, "This is getting monotonous!" She also noticed that Rachel wasn't letting any grass grow under the truck as she sped toward the ranch that had become home base for the team of researchers. "Team of researchers." It was still hard to realize that after the initial months of research, field work, and then the compilation of her master's project work, spurred by the seemingly now distant death threat, she had not only been awarded her Master's Degree, by the governor no less, but was given the full backing of the university to select and monitor a team of one hundred research assistants to continue the research into the source of the toxic contamination of California's west Central Valley's groundwater, that had been released by the 8.0 earthquake along the west side of Interstate 5. Part of her initial findings had started a real evidentiary trail toward a conglomerate that operated a toxic waste storage facility. Her main focus had been refined during the research process to find and test a process through which the valuable land resource could be decontaminated and put back into production. The press conference that followed the special ceremony at which she was recognized, had been successful almost beyond what she could have dreamed, and over five hundred extremely well qualified candidates answered the call for well-qualified student scientists to serve as researchers. As a result, she had a "dream team," which had been in the field for almost a month and was already gathering some very enlightening data.

Stephanie was brought out of her reverie by Rachel's liberal use of the truck's horn as they went through the gate, rattled over the cattle guard, and started up the small grade and around "Ear Rock," a time and weather sculptured, broken pinnacle of rock, which protruded skyward from the surrounding grass of the immense property which lay inside the outer wrought iron gates of the ranch.

"Ouch, that hurt!" Stephanie said ruefully, as the truck bumped over a pothole in the road. She was surprised at her own voice because she hadn't realized that, not only had she spoken out loud, but that her head throbbed as well!

Research team members and ranch hands who were within earshot had started running even before they determined the stopping point of the pickup. When it stopped, sending a small cloud of dust in front of it, a sizeable crowd had gathered outside the large tent which was set up on the front yard of the ranch house. A "beehive" of voices buzzed, but silenced, as a young man strode hurriedly from the ranch house. He approached the pickup, saw who was driving, who was in the passenger seat, and that his wife had a handkerchief to her head.

Ethan's soft, yet firmly controlled voice preempted the buzzing that was about to burst forth again from those gathered, with a simple, "First things first! When I know, you'll know!" Then, opening the truck door, he scooped Stephanie from the seat, and as he did so, he couldn't help wincing just a bit. The wounds that he had incurred protecting her from an assassin just outside the university science building were almost healed, but as he carried his wife into the house, his wound that was still healing, seeped and the blood stained his shirt.

Forty-five minutes later, outfitted with a fresh shirt, he returned to the group which had now been brought up to date by Rachel and had also waited with her to find out Stephanie's condition.

Ethan gave them what facts he had learned and then said, "Team, I have made Stephanie as comfortable as I can. Apparently she had a bullet graze to the head. I've called for the doctor to come and give her a complete check-up. She wanted me to tell you to knock off for the rest of the day, stay close to the house, each other, or the big tent. As a precaution, I'm going to post extra guards tonight. Oh, by the way, don't be too concerned if you see my ranch hands stringing some lights. I figured it would be a good idea to be able to see anyone who might decide to give us a late night visit. One more thing, Stephanie wanted me to be sure to tell you. She will see you in the morning, and if there is anyone who decides by then that this incident makes the job more than what you had bargained, there will be no one to say the worse of you. She just asks that you wait until the morning, so that she can talk to you personally."

The "beehive" disbursed a bit back toward the clean circle of smaller tents that started on one side of the big tent, then stretched out and around, and ended at the other side of the big tent. Some of the "bees" guided Rachel to the big tent where they could get other details from one of their own.

In the background of the circle of tents was the rising frame of a larger version of the ranch hands' bunkhouse, which was meant to replace the temporary tents. The new 'bunkhouse' had been rapidly designed by Ethan, to be, not only the central meeting place and combination research workroom and research laboratory, but also more comfortable living accommodations for the research team. He knew the team would be here, not only to research a method of fixing the contamination, but also of implementing the fix, and that was going to take time.

The dormitory style building was out and away from the ranch house on the north side of the main house, away from the "working" part of the ranch.

When constructed, the "working" part of the ranch had been built downwind of the main house and ranch hand's bunk house. There had been many a time that the inhabitants of the main house, as well as the bunkhouse, had been thankful for that forethought. In Ethan's design, the new "bunkhouse" was placed where it was to give the whole group of structures a balanced look.

Ethan's simple design of the exterior was modeled like the replacement bunkhouse that he had helped his father design and build after the original ranch hand bunkhouse had been heavily damaged by the falling pinnacles of rock during the last earthquake.

The teams' bunkhouse was to be large enough for the one hundred members of the team, and was designed in such a way that the sleeping quarters were behind the main meeting rooms, keeping the visual footprint from overshadowing the ranch house. Some even said the three buildings sort of mimicked the three hills which dominated the background and were represented by the wrought iron work above the ranch gate.

After the excitement had abated, the work resumed on the now even more crucially needed structure. Later, the clean woody smell of freshly cut lumber lingered, after the construction had ceased for the day.

In the dusky air of the fast approaching close of the summer evening, the "blood red" sun seemed to quiver in the heated air as it began its quick descent behind the hills.

In one tent after another, gasoline lanterns started their unmistakable whir, and one after another, the temporary lights which had been placed by the ranch hands in a circle around the tents, came on with their flickering glow. Ethan had directed that the lights be placed far enough away from the tents to not be bothersome, but close enough that no dark shadows were between the lights, the tents, or the house. The lights were connected to a large generator which had been placed as far out of earshot from the tents and house as possible, but still close enough to fully illuminate, so that no one could approach without being seen by the armed ranch hands who Ethan had posted for security.

Chapter Three

Increased Security

Ethan brought the research team up to date and arranged with his foreman to set up the lights, and to post the ranch hands as security. He then came back into the ranch house and asked for, and received, Stephanie's permission to bring the university chancellor up to date. But before he made the call, he made sure that his wife was as comfortable as possible. It was only then that he went into his office and called the chancellor's office. It took some doing, but his persistence finally got him connected with the chancellor at his home. The story told, Ethan asked for the chancellor's advice.

"Ethan, I want to thank you for bringing this to my attention! As soon as I get off the phone, I am going to call Professor Daniels, the head of the science department, and then I'm going to call the governor. The chancellor knew the value of Stephanie to the university, as well as the fact that it was a university sponsored research team at her ranch. Can you be reached at this number this evening?"

"All night, Chancellor. I've got guards outside and I'll be on guard inside! Therefore, I won't be far from the phone."

It was then that the chancellor phoned the governor. "Governor, I'm sorry to break into your evening this way, but I just got a call from Ethan

Carson, the husband of Stephanie Carson. Do you remember Stephanie, the young graduate student who has begun that important study of the toxic contamination of the ground water in the western Central Valley? Oh, good, and by the way, thank you for coming to present her with her Master's Degree! Her husband, Ethan, just called me. Stephanie was shot and wounded this afternoon when she was monitoring a member of the team of graduate students who the university commissioned to help her with her work. Right now, Ethan has his ranch hands patrolling the research compound at their ranch, and he is on guard as well. Given the importance of the team's work, is there anything you, as governor, can do, especially in the way of security?"

"Chancellor, I want to thank you for calling me. I'm going off the phone right now and consult with my team. Will you be at this number for the next hour? Good. As soon as I find out what I can legally authorize, I'll call you!"

For the chancellor, who was used to the day's events happening in rapid succession, suddenly the time seemed to creep by. He was startled by the phone's ring.

"Chancellor?"

"Yes, Governor!"

"Here is what we are going to do! First, I am going to send in some Highway Patrol Officers from Fresno County! I know that in the more rural counties our highway patrol officers are well known, so instead of sending them from the stations closer to the Carson Ranch, we are going to send officers from stations that are further from the ranch, and hopefully will not be so well known! The Fresno County Highway Patrol has already been notified and should be at the Carson's within the hour. Second, I am authorizing a battalion of National Guard Military Police from Fairfield to be called up and be on station for the duration of the research. If need be, we will rotate battalions! I wasn't kidding when I said I thought Mrs. Carson's research to be absolutely vital to the concerns of California. But, Chancellor, no matter how important, there are some political realities. You know I cannot do this indefinitely, don't you?"

"Yes, Governor, I do!"

"Call the Carson's, talk to the team of researchers, tell them we support them, and get as much research out of them as you can, in as short a time as you can. We not only need the 'smoking gun,' the 'bullets,' the 'shooter,' and the 'bankers.' We need the remedy for fixing the problem. I know that is a tall order, but if I am going to sell the expense for the security, let alone the expense for the 'remedy,' I'm going to have as much of that research data as I can get, as fast as I can get it! Do you understand?"

"As you say, Governor, that is a tall order. I'm going to call them now, but I will drive down there tomorrow and deliver the pep talk myself!"

"Excellent, Chancellor, I think you understand what is at stake!"

Ignorant of what was going on outside the ranch house, let alone in Davis and Sacramento, Stephanie rested. Her head throbbed. The realization of what had happened that day began to sink in and she began to tremble with shock. Even as she did so, she tried to come to grips with what had happened.

When Ethan returned to the bedroom, he saw Stephanie's tremors and pulled knitted Afghans from the closet and bundled her to fight the shock induced cold. Even in his haste, he made sure to put the afghan that Stephanie's mother had knitted, and thus Stephanie's favorite, on top of the pile, in an effort to comfort her.

Stephanie's teeth chattered as she smiled in appreciation, and said, "I'm so cold, what is the matter with me?"

Ethan responded, "It's your body coming to grips with shock. We'll keep you warm until the doctor comes to give you a full check up!"

It was perhaps thirty minutes before the doctor could arrive, since his office was in Coalinga. Ethan's family doctor's office was in Hanford. Ethan had determined that waiting for him would take too long, so he called a doctor whose office was closer and whom his family had used before for emergencies.

The Fresno Highway Patrol arrived at the big wrought iron gate just enough ahead of the doctor to stop him and require identification. Therefore, it was a little over an hour and a half from the time Rachel had driven onto the ranch compound with Stephanie, and the doctor having finished dressing Stephanie's wound and giving her a sedative to calm her anxiety.

"Ethan, you did the right thing by calling me. Her wound is not overly serious, and you did all the right measures until I could get here, but untreated, both the wound and the shock could have been much more serious! The best thing for her now is rest, but if her condition changes, do not hesitate to call me!"

"Thank you, Doctor, for coming so quickly. My parents always talked well of you!"

"I don't know if you were aware of it, Ethan, since you were away at the time, but it was I who was called to this house after your father's murder. I am so glad that Stephanie did not suffer his same fate!"

"You are right, Doctor. I did not know. Perhaps when all of this excitement calms down we can talk about that visit and what you found? Let me walk you out to your car and make sure that my ranch hands know who you are!"

"That is appreciated Ethan. I had to identify myself down at the gate on the way in!"

Chapter Four

Reordered Priorities

Late in the morning of the next day, once the chancellor had arrived and the pleasantries were over, he addressed the assembled team.

"You know that the university authorized Stephanie to form this team to do just exactly what she has been doing, and I might add, doing well! You also know that yesterday the opposition raised the ante. I know, I know, we all are pretty sure we know who the opposition is, but until you can prove it, we're stuck. Yes, I said you! If you can prove it, you can give the governor the proof she needs to authorize the appropriate action. Then, and only then, can we proceed with what many of you feel is the more important task, determining the process, and then initiating that process for reclamation of the land for production. I confess that is my feeling as well, but I also know the politics, and politics says for right now that we have to do the first, in order to be able to do the second! Will you do it? Can you do it?"

"Chancellor, since I started this thing, I guess it is up to me to give you some sort of answer," stated Stephanie. Her head bandaged and still a bit groggy from the sedative, Stephanie answered a bit hesitantly. Then, as if gathering conviction, or perhaps it was because Ethan had his arm around her shoulders, her back stiffened with resolve, and she continued more strongly, "I can't, or perhaps a better phrase is, I won't, presume to answer for the team. They can answer for themselves. I started this research because I was concerned about the land, but more than that, I was concerned about who the products grown on this land could, and indeed had, fed and clothed. I was also concerned for the people who live on this land and made producing those products for their neighbors their life's work, mission, and calling. So Chancellor, I can't promise I can find all of what you and the governor have said you need. What I can promise is that I will harness the minds of all those who choose to stay and all those minds that I can find to use from around the world, in the effort you have been honest enough to outline. So Chancellor, you can count me in, bum head and all!"

As had happened once before, it took a minute for the gathered audience to grasp the depth of understanding shown by what the young woman had just said. Then, as if controlled by a single mind, the entire tent full: team members, security, ranch hands and even the chancellor, stood and cheered!

"Does this mean everyone's in?" asked the chancellor.

"Yes!" the response was loud, clear, and unmistakable!

"Ethan, may I use your phone? I want to call the governor," stated the chancellor.

"Yes, Sir, right this way!" was Ethan's immediate answer.

"The battalion of National Guard Military Police will be there tonight," stated the governor. Chancellor, by the way, do the Carson's have the kind of ranch in which the National Guard will have enough room for the entire company, headquarters, vehicles, and communication equipment to set up camp?"

"Governor," the chancellor answered with a chuckle, "They would have enough room if you sent a regiment!"

Chapter Five

Protection Arrives

It had been Stephanie's reluctant, but she knew, necessary, decision to keep the team in the compound until the National Guard Military Police arrived, got set up, and then developed a satisfactory strategy for security, as well as the research, agreed upon. However, not wishing to waste precious time, her instructions to the team had been simple this morning.

"Record and classify any data that is not in the data bank and be sure to back up your research on the separate hard drives. Many of you know that the necessity for separate backups was an important lesson that I learned during my research. I don't want you to have to learn it the hard way. I want you to use our temporary T1 line to the university and back up your data there, but I also want it backed up on our server here, as well as on your back up hard drive, and laptop. I know that many of you might think that this is a little paranoid, but humor me, and do it anyway! This would also be a good time to share with me anything which you think you have found that would advance our understanding of what the chancellor has said the governor needs. I'll be here in the main tent, or in the house. Oh, one more thing, and I know I've said this before, and I know you all have curious family and friends, but nobody, and I mean nobody, says anything about the findings of our research to anyone. You all heard the importance of politics in this thing! When we release anything, we will release it together and everyone's name will be on the report, but only when we are sure of our research!"

It was later, but not long after noon, when a deep-throated rumble of big engines startled Stephanie from her concentration, and she looked down the hill to see a whole line of large, camouflage-painted, military vehicles just barely passing under the wrought iron arch over the gate. The line of dark exhaust fumes wound up the hill around "Ear Rock," as well as the two other fallen pinnacles of stone toppled by the last earthquake.

The now broken pinnacles had been huge monoliths which had been seemingly carried from some other location, and then carelessly dropped in disinterest by some gigantic hand in ancient time, because they did not resemble any other rock formations in the area. The last earthquake had not only caused the great stone formations to fall, but according to Stephanie's preliminary research, had caused the toxic waste disposal facilities containment structures to crack, to leak, and to poison the groundwater, and thus, the land.

"That earthquake damage inspired my research, indirectly led to my marriage, and then my Master's Degree. That 8.0 sure shook things up, in more ways than one!" Stephanie commented silently with an inner smile.

As the first vehicles reached the inner compound, Stephanie saw Ethan directing them to the part of the vast site that he had selected for them, a place that was behind a small ridge just high enough to effectively hide them from the main compound just below. Once again, that now increasingly familiar feeling of loving gratitude filled her as she watched her man, not only in charge of an ever increasingly complex logistical task in support of her and her research, but now turning their much loved ranch into a parking lot for belching beasts. She silently resolved to thank him again tonight!

The ground of the compound shook with the impact of the large wheels and the air was soon foul with the exhaust from their engines. She was glad, when one after another, the engines were shut down and the camouflage suited men and women, descending from their perches high above, were formed up and given instructions in a crisp staccato voice by the woman commander in charge.

After issuing instructions to her unit, she approached Ethan and said in a more mild tone, "Thank you, Sir. The area that you selected seems well suited to our needs!"

Since she was in charge of the research project, which the National Guard came to protect, Stephanie stepped forward and extended her hand. Her voice and her hand testified of both her recent wound and her desire to recover from it. "Welcome. I'm Stephanie Carson, and this is my husband, Ethan. We are glad you are here, so that we can continue our task in more safety. Would you care to join us in the main tent where we can outline our purpose and your role in it?"

"Thank you, Ma'am. My instructions were pretty brief, 'Git' there, do what needs doin',' fast, and git' back home!' There were a few frills and dressins's, but that kind of sums them up!"

Stephanie smiled. She hadn't known up to now, but she thought she was going to like this no-nonsense commander.

For an hour, more or less, the commander, whose name was Leigh, listened to Stephanie, then stood and stretched. It had been a long truck ride from Fairfield, and then this briefing. She said, "Stephanie, and thank you. By the way, your name sounds much better than Ma'am. We will do what we can to provide security, but when it comes to the security of you and your team, will you agree to abide by my suggestions? I'll try to make them suggestions, but there may be times when there won't be time for niceties. Will you agree to my terms?"

Stephanie looked at Ethan, whose face had clouded in concern during this last question. "Ethan, what's troubling you?"

"Well, I guess it's this, you are my wife, this is your team, and this is our land. I feel that the responsibility for all of that is mine, and when someone, anyone, no matter how well intentioned, wants to supersede me, I get, well, nervous."

"Well said, young man! How about this? My primary authority for security will be for your wife and team in the field. Should the occasion arise for action on your land, I will, baring immediate threat, consult you for agreement on my action plans! Will that make you more comfortable?"

"Some," Ethan smiled, "Thank you for understanding!"

"Frankly, Ethan, I would have thought less of you if you hadn't spoken up! Now, I better go give the troops 'the skinny!'"

The team, who had been hovering not far from the tent, didn't need any coaxing when Stephanie motioned them inside to give them, "the skinny."

"We begin tomorrow! I know that some of you have real doubts about 'collaborating with the military,' but if we want to get the job done, and get it done safely, it's got to be done! So, one more time, I'm going to ask if you have enough reservations that you don't think you can do this. Now is the time to say something, with nothing held against you in my records. But if you agree to continue, I don't want to hear any grumbling about having to work with the military. Are there any questions? Ok, hearing none, tomorrow we begin again. Do your job and if your security person should say, 'jump, or hit-the-dirt,' or whatever, do it! Don't start a debate, just do it, and be thankful that you have someone watching out for you! I know, I know, that does not come naturally to academics like us, but do it anyway!"

Chapter Six

Washington Interest

Out of curiosity, Leigh had lingered outside the tent to hear what the young woman leader would say. She had found it useful in the past to know what the people with whom she would be working, told their staff. She was pleasantly surprised at the depth of understanding that Stephanie had demonstrated and the kind of support she could expect from her as her opposite number.

"I don't know how this operation will end, and I don't know if she will be able to accomplish the job with which she has been tasked" she thought to herself, but she liked this girl, and liked her spunk. "I hope she can do it," she said. "I haven't been able to say that, and mean it, for a long time!"

Leigh Hunnecutt started her walk back toward the military encampment. She hadn't known how to communicate with these young academics and when the homespun phrases of her grandfather's movie characters received a warm reception, she decided to keep using them for the time being. She had used some literary license in the story of her orders. Yes, they had been brief, but they had been very specific. She was to do everything within her considerable power to make sure these young scientists were able to conclude their work.

Some powerful voices from the states' and the nation's capitals were reviewing the whole toxic contamination incident. It was true that few people in the nation's capital had previously cared a great deal about this part of California, but when an obscure young graduate student got threatened, followed by the murder of a prominent rancher, who just happened to be the soon to be father-in-law of the same scientist, followed shortly thereafter by still another attempt on the young scientist's life, which resulted in the wounding of her boss, influential backroom Washington heads began to take interest.

Now that the scientist was out of the state's capitol and back researching toxic poisoning in the field, and had another nearly successful attempt on her life, the phone and computer lines between Sacramento and Washington had started humming. A very discreet, but in depth investigation had begun, with no possibilities, including foreign eco-terrorism within the United States, being ignored.

In addition, a new, more in-depth examination was opened on the real money interests that were bankrolling the conglomerate which had taken over the toxic waste facility against which Stephanie's initial research had proved so damaging.

Perhaps this latest shot at Stephanie had not been heard around the world, but it had definitely peaked the interest of some very important, behind the scenes people, and the departments over which they had operational control.

Yes, it had been the California governor who had authorized the California National Guard unit's mobilization to reestablish the serenity of this West Valley ranch, and to keep it that way, but the mobilization would not have been done so expeditiously without the approval of those heads in Washington who were now bringing their attention and considerable authority to bear on this rural part of Central California. Of course, she hadn't told Stephanie and Ethan all of this. There was no sense scaring them when there was nothing to be gained. There might well be a time to do that, but not this evening. Her ruminations ended when she reached the military bivouac and she called to her first sergeant, "Sergeant, will you assemble the platoon and squad leaders, here in ten? Thank you!"

"Yes, Ma'am, right away!" Sergeant Jack, as he was known, knew an order when he heard it, and he did not waste time, but went in a quick walk to each person requested, and relayed it!

In precisely ten minutes, all personnel requested were present and accounted for.

"Very good, Sergeant, thank you! Some of you people are old hands with me and know my expectations. For others, this is our first action together." She saw a few eyebrows raise just a trifle and suppressed a smile. "Yes, you heard me right. I said action; this is no practice field exercise." Here is the situation; we are here at the express order of the governor to provide security for the young scientists who you will meet tomorrow. One of them, the young woman who is the leader, has already survived two attempts on her life!

A ghost of a whistle escaped the lips of one of the assembled leaders.

"Yes, you may well respond!" she said, instead of the reprimand that had risen in her throat. "We are to keep as low a profile as possible. There will be no weekend passes anywhere, partly because there is hardly anywhere to go, and partly because we want as few people as possible to know we are here. You probably noticed we didn't come through or stop in any towns. You will find out tomorrow anyway, that there are nearly as many scientists, as we have assets, so we are going to be spread thin. You have all had a chance to scope out the territory by now, and you have seen that there is a lot of it, and it is mostly fairly flat. The hills to the west will be part of our perimeter, but our main task is to secure the people and they are going to be out 'in the middle of nowhere,' taking soil samples, sub soil readings, and God knows what else! Potential danger will then be possible from all points of the compass. There will be no safe zone when you are in the field! By the way, both previous attempts have been from a distance, just how far a distance has yet to be determined. Any and all people you may meet other than the team, will be potential hostiles. Do you read me?"

"Yes, Ma'am!"

"Good! Sergeant. The rancher on whose land we are a guest, is the husband of the head of this team of researchers and he has had their ranch hands providing security ever since the second attempt on his wife's life. I'll bet that he, and they, would appreciate a break. Will you and the platoon and squad leaders set up a healthy security patrol schedule? You probably saw that huge outer gate and then up the hill, closer to the living quarters, the inner gate. There is no way that we have the man-power to secure the whole property, so we will have to focus on the perimeter made by the inner fence. I believe that is what the ranch hands have been doing, and it is a good plan, so we will use it, at least at first. We are here to provide security, and I aim to do just that! Oh, and one other thing, people, don't screw up! I don't want the scientists or you dead! Got it?"

"Yes, Ma'am!"

"I hope you do! That is all! Sergeant?"

"Yes, Ma'am?"

"I don't intend for this to be a cold camp, at least not yet, but let's keep the fires limited to the gasoline stoves. I meant it when I said I want a low profile. No campfires! Right?"

"Got it, Ma'am!"

"That ought to give them something to talk about tonight!" Leigh murmured, as she turned to write up her report of the day's events. "Tomorrow, I want to look at the bullet strike on that pickup! Sometimes, if you're real lucky, the size can give you a clue about who you are up against, or at least what type of weapon they use. Another item that she had left off the agenda of the chat with Stephanie and Ethan was the nature of the shot that had nearly killed her. It had been a head shot. No amateur thug for hire would even think about that. If Stephanie hadn't stooped to wipe her boots, well, I wouldn't have had the pleasure of meeting her."

The commander wanted to visit where it happened, not because she thought she would find any evidence. She wouldn't, but because she wanted to see what vantage points might have been used to make the shot. Sometimes there is a pattern, but if this assassin was the kind of professional whom she was beginning to get the feeling that he was, there wouldn't be one, but it had to be checked! With that, she yawned, and said, "Tomorrow is another day, I'm bushed!"

Chapter Seven

Rechecking Data

One of the things that Ethan did, after the National Guard had taken over the security perimeter, had been to contact his old FFA buddies who had allowed Stephanie to work in their fields in the first place. After the Guard had taken over perimeter security, Ethan had walked out to the Guard's bivouac area and had asked permission from the commander to confidentially tell just his friends who had originally allowed Stephanie on their land, about the heightened security. The original threats to Ethan's friends had been real enough to make them insist that Stephanie remove her equipment from their land earlier that spring. A few friends had allowed the team back on their land, once they heard about what Stephanie had been commissioned to do, some others because they knew Ethan's Dad, and were angered at his murder. It had been on some of this land that Stephanie and Rachel were studying, when the most recent attempt was made on Stephanie. More than one farm owner friend of Ethan's had lost pets and prized animals in the previous effort to influence them to stop Stephanie's work on their land. Ethan hoped that with the reassurance of security, more of his friends would agree to let the team back on their land.

The commander had been hesitant to grant permission at first, until Ethan explained that, with the additional land to revisit and get updated data, Stephanie and her team might well be able to reach their objective sooner.

After their chat with the team and Ethan's phone calls, Stephanie and Ethan looked at the grid map of land upon which they had been given permission to research. The waste facility was marked, along with radiating arcs from that facility marked with the readings of the various chemicals and toxins that had been established by Stephanie in her previous research. It was reconfirmed that the first thing that had to be done was to finish rechecking those study sites to verify the readings and to see if there had been any change in percentage of toxicity or depth of toxicity. That, of course, was one of the primary fears, namely, that the depth of toxic poisoning would have increased. If that were the case, the principle hypothesis, that the poisons could breach the natural caliche filter layers of the subsoil, and ultimately poison the huge aquifer that lay below would be supported.

Each researcher had been given a copy of their particular part of the study. This had been at the suggestion of the commander, who was frank enough to say that if one researcher were taken who had the entire map, the rest of the team was put in greater danger.

Later, after dinner and after the sun had set, Stephanie fulfilled the promise that she had made earlier to herself to thank her husband in a way that was enjoyable to both of them.

Chapter Eight

Toxicity Increased

The young scientists and their security team had rolled out through the gate early, in an effort to beat at least some of the heat that broiled down from the sun and radiated up from the gray, untilled, and increasingly hardpan, earth. Now there was no sense tilling the earth, since everything that came up was, at least so far, genetically altered to a toxic level. Indeed, that was part of the team's task, to see if there was some process that could slowly decrease the toxicity. Stephanie's research had opened up some tantalizing possibilities, but now that part of the research had to take second place to the plan that the governor had the chancellor present.

That night, after the team and their escort returned from their field work, what would have taken Stephanie by herself weeks or months to test, was entered into the various data banks. The big tent had been set up so that each research scientist had their own station equipped with laptop and backup hard drive. All of the laptops were networked to a joint server and a printer.

The composite report print out was grim. In every case where Stephanie had collected and entered previous data, the new data was worse. Although time should have, through natural processes, diminished the toxicity, there was little, if any, decrease in toxicity, and there was a slight, but measureable increase in depth.

There was something else, just a hint that Stephanie saw, but didn't voice out loud to the team, but saved for Ethan and the commander. Once the team had drifted away, she motioned to the commander and the three of them went to the house. She could tell that Ethan was curious, but the commander was new enough that if she saw it, she was patient enough to let Stephanie tell it in her own time.

"Ethan, Commander, did you see the data that showed no decrease in toxic levels?"

An almost simultaneous, "Yes," came from both of the people addressed.

"Here is the reason I called you here, Commander, Ethan. I know you were curious when I asked you to come up, Commander. It would seem likely, don't you agree, that after a spill of any type, there would be a time of "mess," and then a gradual lessening of degree of contamination."

"That seems logical," Ethan said.

The commander nodded in agreement.

"Then here is my question. Why has there been no natural, perhaps slight, but measureable, decrease in toxicity, while simultaneously there has been a slight increase in depth of contamination?"

A shock of intuition spread over both their faces, "There is a continuing source of toxic material!"

Stephanie nodded. "I think that is what our research findings of today have supported! In fact, if you look at these particular readings, and she indicated the tests done closest to the waste facility, you will notice that on those test sites, there is the greatest increase in toxicity and depth!"

"I'm sorry to interrupt Stephanie, but I think there is someone who needs to hear this right now. May I use your phone?"

Seconds, not minutes later, the commander said, "Governor, I think you need to hear this. I am here with Stephanie and Ethan and no one else. I'm going to put you on speaker. Stephanie, will you please tell the governor what you believe your studies today have supported?"

With as little drama as she just had shared with the two, she shared the findings with the governor.

"Stephanie, you don't disappoint, do you? Security for one day and you have some potentially very important information! Please continue your plan of research. I ask just one modification. In one week, recheck your test sites of today. I'm no scientist, Stephanie, but does that seem a logical way to recheck today's data?"

"Governor, perhaps when you finish being governor, you could join us in science!"

The governor chuckled, and then got serious. "Commander, thank you for bringing this to my immediate attention! Will you please continue to do so?"

"Yes, Ma'am," was the immediate reply, and there was a salute in the tone.

"Stephanie, as much as I know that this is not your natural way, will you please keep your conclusions about today's data as confidential as you can? I would like the team to stay focused on the considerable tasks that I have already outlined and not get involved in speculation, at least for as long as possible. Oh, and by the way, I will see that the chancellor is brought up to speed."

"As you say, Governor, that is not my natural way, but I can see the logic in it, at least for a while."

"Fair enough! Commander, thank you again!"

"Ok, Commander, I don't know "beans from cornbread" about the military, Stephanie snorted, "but that line you gave us, what was it, 'Git' there, do what needs doin,' fast, and git' back home, ' is beginning to sound a little, to put it nicely, disingenuous, don't you think!"

"Ok, you got me," the commander chuckled, "but I was, and still am, under orders, but I'll tell you what I can!"

Ethan, who was winding up to being angry if Stephanie didn't get what she wanted, said a muffled, "bout time!"

"Stephanie, Ethan, you know the Feds came in, paid some damage money after the big earthquake, and left with their checkbooks, right? Well, they thought they got off cheap and didn't think much more about it until an obscure article showed up in the *Science Review,* which began to make a few people nervous within the beltway around Washington. Next, a man got murdered in his home, this home, right? Then a graduate student who just happened to have done the research for that *Science Review* article, and just happened to be the soon-to-be daughter-in-law to the murdered man, published some very interesting findings, and right away she was almost murdered. Finally, the same science researcher who had been honored with a Master's Degree before her project was even finished, unheard of, by the way, was given a huge research grant by the governor of the state and was promptly almost murdered again. When the governor of that state was called and told that the person who she had honored was almost murdered again while doing a job that she, the governor of one of the most influential states in the country, authorized. What do you think happened in Washington when she called some very important people? All of a sudden, some lights that generally don't go off until very late in the offices of people who are paid to be paranoid, didn't go off at all!"

Stephanie and Ethan, who had lived it, and had never thought about it in just those terms, looked at each other with a bit of disbelief on their faces. Then, the realization came that this military person who was sitting in their living room, who had purported to know little of the situation, all of a sudden, knew an awful lot about their business.

Leigh saw it in their eyes, and recognized it because she had seen it before. "You didn't really think that the governor and our commanding officer would send us into the field without knowing the parties with whom we would be dealing? That only happens in the movies! I can't tell you much more yet, other than, that all of a sudden, some government financial types are doing some very discreet, but in-depth, research into the financial resources of the conglomerate that you mentioned which purchased the waste facility."

Stephanie's innate sense of logic conquered her apprehension. "But the release was triggered by the earthquake and that could have been, well, anytime or never."

"First, isn't it part of your job to prove the first part of that last assertion?"

Stephanie felt her color rising, the blush phenomenon that she had thought she had conquered. "Of course but…!"

"As for the second part, there are forces in the world that understand, perhaps better than some people in Washington, the importance of the production, or lack of production capabilities of this valley. Would you agree?"

"Definitely," replied both Ethan and Stephanie simultaneously.

Commander Hunnecutt continued, "Frankly, I probably exceeded my orders in the scope of what I have shared with you tonight; but one, I thought you ought to know; and two, if I have to make some security decisions on your behalf, I thought if you knew a little more, those measures might be a little easier to swallow! It may be that what we have here is a case of corporate greed gone really nasty, or it may be something a lot more sinister."

Ethan, would you support me if I were to suggest that Stephanie is too important to this research to risk "in the field?"

"Definitely!" Ethan answered with a certain set to his jaw.

Just as Stephanie was about to protest, she saw that jaw, and knew better! Ethan didn't look that way often, but when he did, even though they hadn't been married very long, she knew it would be no use! She settled for a grumbled, "Oh, all right, if you insist!"

Chapter Nine

Another Attack

The next three days passed uneventfully, except that as the team fanned out around the arcs on that grid map, the same results came back, little or no reduction of toxicity, greater depth of contamination, with the only respite in bad news being that the outward radius of contamination, although miles in measurement, had not increased dramatically, but was relatively stable. It looked somewhat like a flattened half circle, approximately fifty miles in diameter and perhaps ten to fifteen miles deep at the right angle. Part of the puzzle that the team was trying to piece together was why the disbursement was not more evenly distributed.

On the fourth day, as the team's assignments took them further away from the origination point, and further from base camp, the routine of the last few days changed. The communications technician arrived on the run to the commander's tent.

"Ma'am, excuse me, Ma'am!"

"Yes, Private?"

"We just had a communication from one of our people which was broken off in mid transmission!"

This breech of protocol caused the fine hair on the back of the commander's neck to tingle.

"Show me!"

All calls from the testing sites were routinely recorded, and it had taken the commander, followed by the private, only a minute or two to return to the communications tent. When they arrived, the private hit the play switch.

"Home base, this is station ten. We've got troub…" and although the carrier signal from the remote radio was still sending, the voice transmission ended.

"Private, try to reestablish contact. I'll be at the big tent."

The commander crossed the distance from the bivouac area to the big tent on the double.

"Stephanie, excuse me. May I speak to you quickly?"

The commander's sudden arrival and interruption of a team consultation got an immediate reply.

"Of course, what is it?"

"Who is your team member at station ten, and where exactly are they?"

"That would be Rachel. She and her security detail are the furthest team to the north. Why?"

"Please show me on the map."

Stephanie pointed to the research field about fifteen miles north and about five miles east.

In hushed tones, the commander told her what she knew.

"We've got to go find out! Stephanie responded, already turning to go.

"Wait a minute. I thought we agreed you weren't leaving this area!"

"But she may be hurt!" Stephanie couldn't help remembering that it was Rachel who had brought her home after she had been wounded.

"We are trying to re-establish communications, but if we haven't by the time I get back to the communications tent, I will send a reconnaissance in force team, since we don't know what we might find. You and your team will stay here, and I will issue orders for all stations to return to base immediately. The reconnaissance in force will consist of three armored humvees and the medics. I would like to send a deuce and half, but they are too slow."

Stephanie didn't like having to stay behind, but she knew Ethan wouldn't have let her go.

"Lieutenant, we don't know what is out there, so be vigilant! Your call sign will be 'Ranger One."

"Yes, Ma'am!"

In less than a half hour, the radio crackled in the communication tent.

"Home base, this is Ranger One. Come in!"

"Roger, Ranger One. What's the situation?"

"We are on station, the scientist is dead, and so is our man!"

"Understood! Bring our people back and gather anything that looks like it might be test data or instruments, and get back to home base fast!"

"Roger that! Out!"

In less than forty-five minutes the recon team was back.

"Ok, Lieutenant, report!" The commander was angry and she didn't mind showing it.

"We arrived on station and found our man down, with his fingers still clenched on the call button of his radio. About ten feet away, we found the scientist, just kind of slumped over, like she had been kneeling when she was shot. One more thing, Commander, I found this clenched in the fingers of our man's other hand." The lieutenant held up a camouflage strip from what could only have been a "ghillie suit."

"Well, isn't that interesting! Good report, Lieutenant! I want you to know that my irritation wasn't with you or your team, just the situation! Now, I have to go and tell the people who we were sent to protect what you found!"

"Stephanie, I told you I would tell you what we found out!" The commander then told Stephanie, after Rachel's body and that of her security person had been carefully lifted from the medic's humvee and taken into the impromptu morgue.

The entire research team was back in the big tent, in a state of shock and disbelief. Despite the attempt on Stephanie, until now, the team had had a kind of insulated feeling, combined with an air of superiority, that they were smart enough to outwit the faceless threat. Like the rest of the team, Stephanie was just kind of numb.

"Stephanie, Ethan, may we go to the house? There is something else I want to share with you."

"What, oh sure, come on, Commander."

Once inside with Stephanie and Ethan seated, the commander held up the piece of fabric.

"This is a piece of a 'ghillie suit.' A 'ghillie suit' is an entire body type of camouflage. Although there are cheaper ones for paintball commandos, the material of this one is custom. Only military or ex-military would have, or could afford, a suit of this quality!" the commander said. "Apparently, our man grabbed at the assassin before he died and tore this from him. What that means is that we are up against military or ex-military, a mercenary who is an expert sniper, who may be working alone, or quite likely as part of a team. Oh, and one other thing, Stephanie, the section of map that Rachel took to the site, was not found!"

"Good grief, what have I gotten us into, Ethan?" Stephanie sighed.

Ethan's reaction was to hug her close to him, and she snuggled close in response to his gesture of support for a moment, but then her back stiffened, her face clouded, and the back of her neck flushed, spreading upward until one could almost see steam emanating from her nostrils.

"Ethan," asked the commander, "May I use your phone to make another call to you know who?"

Again the connection was made quickly and the report made.

"Stephanie?" The commander had pressed the speaker button, "I'm deeply sorry for your loss, but what is made evident by this tragedy is that someone is becoming desperate, so you must be getting close! I am going to pass this information along. The commander has told me what she shared of the situation with you. What do you want to do?"

"Governor, what I would like to do is go hide somewhere and cry, but I started this thing, and you know, not until just now did I get really angry. When Ethan's father was killed, we were so wrapped up in doing research and putting pieces together that, what facts there were, didn't really sink in. After the ceremony, there was all the work to do to find and select the team. There really wasn't time to grieve then either. Up to now, I just wanted to solve the puzzle and put the land back into production. But as I was sitting here listening, all of a sudden, all of that hit me. Now, now I am angry and getting even more so, the more I think about it! However, first, I've got to call Rachel's parents and find out what arrangements they want, but when that is over, we are going to finish this thing, and call some people to account!"

Chapter Ten

Another Death

The graveside service had been quickly arranged at the request of Rachel's parents, who, although not orthodox Jews, still honored and kept many of the Jewish traditions. Stephanie got the phone number of their rabbi and called him to see if there were any particulars that they should and could do for Rachel and her family. The rabbi told her what she and the team could do, and what would have to be done when he got there. At the family's request, members of the team had held a vigil with the covered body of Rachel. Stephanie had quickly researched the Jewish prayers for the dead on the internet and those had been said, as much in accordance with Jewish tradition as they had found, until Rachel's parents arrived.

Ethan had offered a portion of his ranch as a grave site. Indeed, it was in that area in which his father had been buried just weeks before. During Stephanie's research, she found information regarding the Jewish tradition of being buried with family and told Ethan, who gladly made provision for the parents and any other family to be buried there as well.

Rachel's parents brought the rabbi. He performed the rites necessary to ready the body of Rachel for the grave, as well as making the ground an acceptable place for the body, according to Jewish law.

Ethan and his ranch hands had refurbished the fence and cleaned the brush from around the burial site after his dad had been buried next to his mother. The fence had been built five years earlier after his mother had died, to protect the site from the many coyotes and other wild animals that inhabited the small hills slightly above and behind the ranch house. His dad had said that it made him feel better to know that his wife was still near and able to look down upon the ranch that she had loved and helped build.

Ethan and his family had not been affiliated with any particular church and so when Stephanie asked if he would like her father, Ray, to conduct the simple ceremony for his father, he had agreed with thanks. Stephanie's father, besides being a pickup restorer, a retired teacher, and a small farmer, was an ordained minister and unpaid pastor of a small community church.

It was after Ethan's father's service that Ethan had been informally welcomed into Stephanie's family. It was true that Ethan had met and brought Stephanie's father to the ceremony in which she was honored with her Master's Degree, but there had been so many things going on then, there hadn't been much time for real talk. It had been after the traditional meal which followed the simple graveside service, that Stephanie's father, Ray, had taken Ethan aside and had a long chat.

It was Ray who had come, at Stephanie's bidding, after the death of Rachel, to do what he could as a grief counselor for her team and Rachel's family. His was a ministry of calm reassurance. It was his down to earth manner and genuine concern that had helped the rabbi comfort the distraught parents, and help initiate the healing process for those team members at the compound.

That afternoon, after they found out the Jewish procedures that Rachel's parents required, prior to her burial, Ethan had gone to the Guard bivouac area and told the commander that he had a rather large refrigerator in the barn and asked if that might be useful for the fallen guardsman.

"Ethan, you continue to impress me! Thank you for your thoughtfulness. We will take care of that as much out of eyesight as we can."

It was after the service of burial that Stephanie made sure to talk privately with Rachel's parents about the personal connection she and Rachel had made after the attempt on Stephanie's life and how it was Rachel who had the presence of mind to get them out of danger.

It was right after the meal that Stephanie had talked to the members of the team, for she knew that Rachel's death had deeply affected all of them. She had left up to each of them the decision to leave, with no recriminations on any graduate records, or stay and finish the job. Later that evening when Rachel's parents and the rabbi left, they were followed by a string of cars and trucks. Many of the team left because they just figured it wasn't worth the risk. By the time the sun went down that day, Stephanie's team of a hundred, had shrunk to sixty-five.

Leigh Hunnecutt had attended Rachel's service and reception in uniform to pay the National Guard's respects, but had stayed in the background, out of the center of attention. She had already had to make arrangements for her murdered team member and his body was lying in a flag draped box inside Ethan's walk-in refrigerator in the barn until a unit dispatched from Fairfield could get there and take it back for appropriate honor. She couldn't spare the vehicle or the man power to send members of her battalion with the body back to Fairfield. She had decided, and her commander back at base had concurred, that it would take longer for a ground honor procession from Fairfield to get there and return with the body, but the faster "Jolly Green Giant" Guard helicopter that was big enough for the body and honor guard to come flying in, land, and take off again, would create unwanted notice on the surrounding farms. There were occasional helicopters in the area and rarely even a "Jolly Green Giant." Except for the helicopter crop dusters, almost all of them were either going to, or coming from, NAS Lemoore, miles east of the Carson ranch.

That evening, after the string of cars and trucks had left, Leigh thought she knew what that sight would mean to Stephanie and felt sorry for the young woman, but at the same time she couldn't help seeing the practical side. Suddenly, there were a whole lot less people for whom to provide security.

"Shame on you!" she murmured, "But it is true, our job just got easier!"

Before Leigh left for the Guard's bivouac, she quietly suggested to Stephanie and Ethan that they have a chat before anything else was done the following day. She still hadn't had an opportunity to check out the bullet strike on Stephanie's pickup, so she made an about face and went to the carport beside the garage, turned on the overhead light and examined the truck. She had heard that Stephanie had suggested sheepishly after she had been attended to by the doctor, that all of this was much ado. Perhaps it just had been a hunter's stray bullet that had clipped her or someone's .22. Leigh finally found the bullet strike. It had hit one of the curved surfaces on the back of the cab on the driver's side and had burrowed a deep, wide groove before veering off. This groove had not been made by a .22 or a hunter's rifle. Unless she missed her guess, this groove had been made by a .50 caliber slug. Considering the depth and width of the groove, only the heavy steel of the old pickup had prevented it from going through. Tied with the ghillie suit, this information gave Leigh a shudder.

"We may be up against an M107 sniper rifle or rifles and people who are skilled in using them!" she said in a whisper, as if even saying it was dangerous. It is quite possible that the person or persons who had killed Rachel and her Guardsman, and wounded Stephanie had been a mile away when they pulled the trigger.

"Whoever has been behind these events has deep pockets and the determination to spend freely from them, to have hired and supplied a force over this much time. Each one of those rifles, if indeed it is an M107, costs over ten thousand dollars. Personnel costs would have already run into the millions of dollars. Whoever it is, they are serious!" Leigh murmured.

"Penny for your thoughts!" Ethan said, startling the commander. He had seen the light and had come to check it out.

Briefly, the commander shared her deductions with Ethan and said, "Perhaps you could let this be just our secret for now, Ethan. I don't think Stephanie is ready to hear it yet."

"You got that right! "Ethan said, and as they turned to leave, he turned off the light in the carport where the old, now "wounded" stepside pickup had been driven after delivering Stephanie to safety.

Chapter Eleven

Communications Leak

The first thing the next morning, after the guard of honor had arrived and left with the fallen soldier, the commander was in the living room with Ethan and Stephanie.

"First, Stephanie, no readings or map data were recovered from the site of the two murders, so we must surmise that the data that was on that part of the map is now compromised," Leigh reported.

Stephanie replied, "It was a good idea of yours to only have the data that each team member needed on their segment of the map."

Leigh continued, "Second, I don't know if you have thought of it yet, but Rachel and my man were quite a ways away from here. Their position in the field and the position of Rachel's body and the guardsman indicate that she was killed from a distance and, although the guardsman was wounded from a distance, he had been close enough to tear the attacker's suit. We theorize that the sniper came in to verify the kills, and that is when our wounded man tore the suit and was finished off by the killer. One question immediately comes to mind."

Stephanie interrupted before she even realized she was doing it. "With all the places that they might have been, how did the sniper know where they would be?"

With a wry smile, the commander thought how nice it would be to work with people who were this sharp. "You are quite correct, Stephanie. In fact, the sniper was probably set up and waiting for just the right moment. How did that happen? You told me that you are out of range of all the cell towers here, so it wasn't necessary to confiscate phones. The only communications that we have monitored since we got here were two high-speed burst transmissions. One was after we got here and got set up, and the other that was monitored was after the team members had left on their various assigned routes this morning. I have already asked my communication wizards to see if they can decipher the encrypted messages."

The conversation was interrupted by a knock on the door, which was answered by Ethan. A guardsman asked to speak with the commander. After their short interchange, the commander came back into the center of the room.

"Third, Ethan I am sorry to say this for many reasons, but the communications people have just deciphered enough to know that the transmissions were from one of your ranch hands, a man named Alex!"

"Why, that's my foreman! I knew he wasn't too happy about women here, especially when they turned out to be in control. My Dad hired him, and I think that he had even invested in the waste management facility when my Dad did."

A call went out for the foreman, and it wasn't long until one of the guardsmen brought him up to the house.

"Ma'am, I apprehended this man as he was trying to leave the compound."

"Good work, Private. I'll take him off your hands so you can return to your post!"

The commander began the questioning of Alex in the living room and, only minutes later, surrounded by the furniture that he had helped Ethan's dad carry in and place, the answers to the commander's questions came.

The story was all too familiar and sad. Alex had invested heavily in the waste management company on advice from Ethan's dad, and when the firm had to pay damages after Stephanie's initial findings, the management had taken the money for the damages from investment dividends rather than a profit/loss fund. As a result, the foreman had lost almost the entire investment of his retirement fund. When the foreman had been approached, he was offered enough money to recoup his losses, and make enough beyond to retire on a small place on which he had made a down payment. When he lost his money, he couldn't pay for the property he had desired, so he lost the property and his down payment. He might not have accepted the money if Ethan's Dad had been alive, but with him dead, the last line of resistance faded when Alex was offered even more money than the initial offer. Rachel had happened to ask him the most direct route to the station to which she had been assigned, and thus the sniper was lying in wait for her to show up and get busy.

"Alex, was it you who gave the information that almost got my wife killed?" Ethan asked with red beginning to flush his neck, despite his tan.

"Mr. Ethan, honest, I didn't think they meant to kill anyone. The way they talked, they just wanted to put a good scare into your wife's people so this whole research project would go away! After Miz' Stephanie was wounded, I tried to give the money and the transmitter back, but they said worse would happen to me, since I had accepted their money, and after all, they just wanted to scare the research people away."

"How did they contact you?" queried the commander.

"After Mr. Carson, Ethan's dad, was laid to rest, Ethan gave each of the ranch hands two hundred dollars, and told us to take the weekend off and have a drink or two in honor of his dad. Well, he didn't have to ask twice, so we all headed to that Indian casino south of Lemoore. I made sure I paid for my room first, so I would have a place to crash, because I knew I was going to have more than a drink or two in honor of Ethan's father and then I went to one of the bars in the casino. The rest of the boys went on to the game rooms. They knew I wasn't a gambler. I got a drink and, to pass the time between drinks, I started to put some money in the slot machines. I wasn't even past my second drink when a couple of guys, and before you ask, no, I'd never seen them before, came up and asked if I'd like to make some real money. I was always told not to look a gift horse in the mouth, but that seemed just a little too good to be true. I told them I might be interested, depending, but that I was willing to listen. As I told you, I did need the money! They asked me over to one of the restaurants where we could talk."

"They told me that they represented certain interests who were interested in getting the research group that was heading my way packed up and sent back where they came from. Those interests would like to have no more meddlesome outsiders, and that included my new boss's wife, stick'n' their noses where they didn't belong, and those interests were willing to pay, to pay me if I was interested, some good money to help make that happen!"

"Miz' Stephanie, I hardly knew you then, and I didn't know then that what you were going to do was to help the people around here, so I agreed! We went to my room and they paid me a pretty sizable down payment. It was enough for me to recover the down payment I had made. They gave me that transmitter gizmo and showed me how to use it. Honest, Miz' Stephanie, I did try to give the money back after you were wounded, but they wouldn't take it. They said wounding you had been a mistake. They had just meant to scare you. Then the National Guard got here and I was really scared. I radioed once to tell them the Guard was here. When I was on guard duty way down by the gate, one of them called me to the fence and said they needed to know when one of the research people was going to be a distance from the compound. They wanted to scare them real good so they would leave. That's when I radioed again about Miz' Rachel goin' way off northeast. Just now, when I heard myself tell it, I wouldn't believe it if someone was telling me, but that's the truth, so help me!"

"Alex, I believe you," Stephanie said.

"Thanks, Miz' Stephanie. Comin' from you, that means a lot!"

"Ethan, do you have somewhere where we can secure Alex?" the commander asked.

"Ma'am, my runnin' is done. You tell me where to sit, and I'll stay put!"

"I think I believe you, Alex, but if others in the compound get wind of what you have been involved in…you catch my drift?"

"Yes, Ma'am, I think I do!" Alex responded, "I hadn't thought of that!" After a moment, he said to Ethan, "How about the old pump house? It is big enough for a cot and it has electricity for a light, and there is a hasp on the door that could take a lock."

With an approving eye, Ethan asked, "How does that sound, Commander?"

"Sounds like it will do for now!"

Once Alex was safely under lock and key, with a few amenities for minimum comfort, Ethan and the commander returned to the house.

Chapter Twelve

Trap Planned

When the two got back to the house, they could sense there had been a change in Stephanie.

"What's up, Hon'?" asked Ethan.

"Well, while you two were gone, I had a minute to assess my behavior of late, and was disappointed in what I found out!"

"Well, good grief, you were wounded, and then one of your team was killed. I'd say you were entitled!" Ethan retorted.

"Thanks for the try, Hon'! But it won't wash! I have been out of it for a while, but I'm back! Commander, did you or your team actually find that transmitter that Alex was using?"

"As a matter of fact, we did, and if you're thinking what I think you're thinking, I'm glad to have you back!" Leigh answered with a grin that was spreading from ear to ear.

"Well, will someone clue me in? I guess I'm a little dense right now!" Ethan responded with just a little irritation.

Stephanie rushed over, hugged him, and said, "If we have the transmitter, perhaps we can send a message and have our own reception committee. Right, Leigh!"

"Definitely right, Stephanie!"

"Whoa! Wait a minute. Won't that be pretty dangerous for the bait who is going to be the lure for your little trap?" interjected Ethan with a rush.

"But if we could catch one or more, think of the potential information we could learn!" Stephanie answered, with just a touch of impatience.

"Stephanie, Ethan is right. It is dangerous!"

"Of course, I'm right!"

"Ethan, Stephanie is right as well!"

Stephanie's look made it unnecessary for her to speak.

Leigh said, "I agree with both of you, but I think the possible gain, at least balances the risk. We have been playing 'catch-up-ball' in this particular 'game' since the beginning. Stephanie's plan, risky as it may be, gives us a chance to get ahead, and let the other team play 'catch-up' for a while."

"Stephanie, you are not going to be the bait, and that's all I have to say at the moment!" Ethan said it quietly, but his jaw was set.

They hadn't been married very long, but one of the things she had already learned about Ethan was that look.

"Ok, Ethan, I won't be the bait!" Stephanie said, just as quietly.

Just after that exchange, Ray, Stephanie's father, after an informal counseling session with some of the remaining team, made his presence known with a hearty, "You'll do son, you'll do! Stephanie knows I am a fan of old movies and that line of 'the Duke's' seems really appropriate here. I wondered if you would be able to hold your own with my daughter, and I see you can. Well done! It looks like you folks have your heads together about something, so I'll not interfere. But before I leave, Commander, I couldn't help noticing your name plate earlier when you had your uniform on. Hunnecutt isn't too common of a California name. You couldn't perhaps be related in some way to a character actor of a few years back?"

A smile spread on Leigh's face when she replied, "I could, and I am. I am proud to say he was my grandfather!"

Her smile was mimicked by Stephanie's Dad, when he replied, "Well, if that don't beat all! You and I are going to have some time to talk about that, when things settle down a mite. What do you say to that?"

"I would enjoy that very much, Mr. Granger, very much indeed!"

"You have made an old man's day, Commander. Well, on that happy note, I will bid you good evening!"

"I was about to say just before that pleasant interruption, that I think I have a solution to the opportunity we were discussing, if you will allow it," Leigh mused.

"I have a guardswoman who is the same general build and hair color as you, Stephanie. Oh, she's not your doppelganger, but there is definitely some similarity. If we were to put her and a guardsman into your red pickup, Stephanie, and have them drive to the spot that we pick and have them begin to work as you would, well, I think we would have the odds on our side. Stephanie, could you give the young woman some general tips on what you might be doing, so she would look like she knew what she was doing for a while."

"Of course, I could, Leigh!"

"Then let's study the map and choose a spot that would seem like a good spot to continue your research as if nothing has happened. In, fact, let's choose three, and once we have three logical choices, then we will pick the best one for our ability to protect our people, and catch some of the opposition!"

"One other thing, Leigh, and it may seem silly, given what is going on, but if at all possible, I would like for my pickup to not sustain any more damage. She is part of the family!"

"I think I understand, Stephanie, and I will pass it along, but my people come first!"

"Of course, Leigh, of course!" but there was a noticeable lack of conviction in her voice.

Leigh couldn't help thinking, "That must be some special truck!"

Chapter Thirteen

Trap Location

The three of them decided on three spots that would be consistent with spreading outward from the compound. The first spot was the right distance, but it was Ethan who said, "The distance may be right, but that is out in the middle of nowhere. Your people would have no place of concealment from which to watch for the snipers."

"Then number one is out, Ethan. How about number two?"

"As far as concealment goes, your people would be able to hide. Unfortunately, so would the snipers. I keep thinking about what you said about the snipers could be as much as a mile away, which would mean your people would have to be more than that or they would be within the line of sight of the snipers."

"Very true Ethan. That makes the area from "the bait" at least a mile in every direction."

Stephanie piped up, "How about this spot? It is close to the aqueduct, which is raised a bit in this area so that any sniper who was on the bank could look down, but they themselves would be visible, and if they were on the other side, they couldn't see "the bait." Wouldn't that effectively narrow the search grid of three hundred sixty degrees by half?"

"You are absolutely right. Are you sure you didn't stick a military strategy class into your class schedule somewhere along the way?" Leigh asked lightly.

"One more thing," and Stephanie had a ghost of the old blush in response to the praise, "A little over a mile west of the aqueduct there is a road, and on the north side of the road there is an orchard from which your people could conceal themselves on the west side. On the east side, there is a building on the bank of the aqueduct that holds test equipment for monitoring the aqueduct. Your people would want to be in there, to not only deny it to the snipers, but to watch from the east side. Oh, and one more thing, on the southwest corner of the intersection, there are often farmers operating a small roadside produce market. Your people could be operating that market as well."

"You've been thinking about this for a while, haven't you?" asked Leigh.

"Well, once we started picking places, this did come to me as a possibility," Stephanie admitted.

"I wish some of my people had the ability to see the situation, not only in three hundred sixty degrees, but in three dimensions, as you just did!"

"Another thing, if your people who were 'the bait' were about a hundred yards south from the road that runs east and west, my truck ought to be out of the line of fire," she added just a bit sheepishly. "The snipers could approach from the north, but that would put a road between them and the target, so it is possible that road would further narrow the search to just a ninety degree approach area."

"You do think things through, don't you?" Leigh said admiringly. "I think I want to set it up for day after tomorrow. That will give my people a full day to get into position. It will give them a cold night, but I don't want any slip ups. I think it is a good idea to have a briefing, as if you were handing out assignments for the next day in case anyone is watching, which they probably are. Then, that night I will have Alex send the message that 'you' are going out in the field the next day because there is an important reading that you want to double check personally."

"Ethan, you know this territory better than I do," Stephanie said. "Is there anything I have left out?" She knew it would be important to Ethan to have a chance to have an opportunity for input.

"You have laid everything out well, Hon,' with the possible exception of one thing. There aren't always farmers with produce at that site. Perhaps I could have a friend I know supply the truck, trailer, and produce, and then leave as soon as your men get there. How does that sound, Leigh?"

"It sounds like a good addition to the plan. Good thinking! Unless anyone can think of anything else, I'll go and brief my people. I want them ready to leave before first light."

Chapter Fourteen

Trap Sprung

Stephanie and Ethan did not sleep well, in anticipation of the beginning of the plan that might bring a stop to the danger and resultant anxiety that everyone was suffering. It was well before first light when the borrowed vehicles were heard to leave.

About thirty minutes after Leigh had left the previous evening, she came back with a suggestion that one of her team had made, that instead of using the very noticeable guard vehicles, they borrow some of the civilian ones, to be a little less noticeable. Both Stephanie and Ethan had agreed and had hurriedly arranged that with some of Stephanie's team.

As had been their habit for the last few days, since the research had been on hold, the team went to the big tent to work on the information that had been gathered. The big map, and of course, all the various data banks that Stephanie had requested, were constantly updated. In addition, the big tent had a section that was devoted to lab work. It hadn't been used much when the team had been in the field, but since that had been suspended, Stephanie had asked that a few of the researchers begin research and testing on the soil samples they had taken, with the purpose of beginning to find the procedures to expeditiously decontaminate the soil.

Another group had been given the task of doing online research on all the previous processes of filtering toxic contaminated water. Stephanie's early research had found some interesting pilot efforts and the team wanted to know all that had been done, so they didn't duplicate research that had already been done.

The laptop stations and their accompanying equipment in the big tent were rearranged to accommodate the new study sub groups and to give the lab a bit more room. Of course, the special challenge that they were facing was the great number of contaminating agents that had been released. Therefore, they were also looking into any research that had been done on a sequence of decontamination on either soil or water.

At the present time, the team had been divided into thirds, with a little over twenty people assigned to each task. It was amazing what twenty people could research, given the kind of internet access, lab equipment, soil samples, and raw data that had been accumulated. The answers didn't come easy, but at least they did begin to come.

Late that afternoon, after the research had been halted for the day, Stephanie called all the team together and gave them an assessment of what the research for the day seemed to begin to show. Anyone who might have been watching could have easily jumped to the conclusion that assignments for the following day were being given.

Thirty minutes later, a now eager to help Alex, sent the radio transmission that had been worked out in advance to set the trap. The commander's people were all in the places that had been worked out by Stephanie, Ethan, and the commander, and had been there for hours.

Once it was fully dark, at about ten o'clock, some of the National Guardsmen thought they caught a glimpse of something moving. The interception team had been issued starlight night vision scopes, which greatly enhanced their ability to see clearly, although it was dark. It was not long until the team members in position to see, saw an attack team of five men, all in ghillie suits and equipped with M107 sniper rifles. The M107 was a weapon that had seen several newer upgrade models, but was still the favorite among professionals.

The attack team moved very slowly and from different compass points, but as Stephanie had projected, all but one approached from the ninety degree quadrant. The fifth man advanced from the north so that he would be looking across the east-west road at the "target." It took them six hours of moving very slowly and deliberately, to get to their selected positions, in an arc that began just west of the aqueduct and south of the east-west road, to the man who was north of the east-west road. All were about three quarters of a mile away from the spot that Alex had radioed that "Stephanie" would be in the morning.

At nine in the morning, Stephanie's red stepside pickup was driven in from the west and parked on the south side of the road about one hundred yards west of the aqueduct. "Stephanie" and her security guard got out, went around to the back, and got the long test probes. They went out into the field about a hundred yards, checked their coordinates, placed their probes, and started to take readings.

When the attack team had each adjusted their windage and leaned to their telescopic sights, a voice sounded loudly through a portable bullhorn.

"This is to the five men poised to fire on the people in the field! Get up and move away from your weapons. Attempt to fire, and you will be fired upon. You should know that you are zeroed in upon by multiple weapons!"

The man who was situated in the arc furthest south made the small move of his finger from the "safety" position toward the "fire" position, and a shot rang out, disabling his weapon and wounding him severely.

"You were told not to move! The rest of you, stand, put your hands on your head, interlace your fingers and move slowly toward the red pickup!"

The second man from the one who had just been wounded started to make a move with his weapon, and at least six shots rang out, cutting him almost completely in half! That immediate and deadly response seemed to take the fight out of the rest of them and they did as they were told.

"Stephanie" and her security team were closest, so they moved to take the men into custody. The man closest to "Stephanie" pulled a pistol from between his shoulder blades and shot and severely wounded "Stephanie." He was killed immediately for his action. The wound, though serious for "Stephanie." was not life threatening.

When the interceptors started toward the "capture point," three shots in rapid succession finished the job on "Stephanie," on her security, and on the nearest guardsman to them. Everyone else in the immediate vicinity of "Stephanie," hit the dirt. Immediately, and from a distance, three return shots were fired, with the impact upon the metal shed on the bank of the aqueduct within seconds thereafter. The reports of the rifle were muted as if from far away. It was then that the rest of the team realized that the man assigned to the building on the bank of the aqueduct had not come out to join them.

Later, Sergeant Jack loped up. It was he who had the most distant position and had returned fire. It was also he who inspected the shed on the bank of the aqueduct. Returning to the group who was gathered around the dead, he asked to speak to the commander privately.

"Commander, our man on the aqueduct was one of our best, yet I found him with his back broken, and garroted inside the building, with no signs of a struggle and his weapon still in his hand. Only a really professional, experienced soldier could have killed him that way. In addition, I found the distinctive marks of a professional garrote on his neck!"

"Thank you, Sergeant. I would appreciate it if you continued to keep this information just between us!"

As far as the stalkers were concerned, the elimination of their teammate and the presence of someone else in the attack scenario seemed to take the life out of the remaining two. The third man, who had been wounded first, was brought up, given some elementary first aid and then questioned. The questions had already begun for the other two and it was not long before a remarkably similar and misleading story began to take shape.

The attackers did not have much to say until they were taken back to the compound, and confronted by the commander, who was none too gentle about wanting information. The attackers were then separated and questioned individually. Although at first, they gave the same prepared misleading information, it was in the nature of the prevarications that the truth began to emerge.

The National Guard military police knew what they could and couldn't legally do in the questioning and they went right up and touched the line, but didn't cross it!

According to the combined story that was constructed from the interrogations, some shadowy figures who said they represented interests in the waste facility had seen the ex-soldiers' names on a mercenary web site, had interviewed, hired, equipped, and told them what they wanted done. The directions were specific and suggested that their superiors would be happy if the targeted individuals were found and eliminated with as much dispatch and prejudice as could be mustered. The mercenaries were given a phone number to call when the job was done, when significant progress had been made, or when they needed additional money or supplies.

At first, the men had been a little slow in getting started and had missed eliminating the young woman while she was in the field months back. They had a little later, however, eliminated the wavering waste management board member, and then were more successful in undermining Stephanie's support by the farmers, by threatening them with intimidation through attacks on their pets and prized animals.

The assassins had almost found and eliminated Stephanie and Ethan outside Auburn after the young couple had bought a new car. The couple disappeared and, although an attempt was made to find them in the area around Auburn, that attempt had not been successful.

In an attempt to get ahead of the young woman and reestablish contact, they figured that the couple would have to return to the university to finish the research report, so they staked out the science building. If it hadn't been for a glass reflection distorting the aim, the young woman and the threat would have been eliminated.

At first, even though the targets hadn't been eliminated, the work they were doing had been slowed significantly, so the employers of the assassins hadn't been overly upset by their continued failure. But when the governor came and presented the young woman with her Master's Degree and the university authorized a massive research project, the pressure on the mercenaries to be successful was intensified with an "or else!" added for good measure, with little doubt left as to what the "or else" meant!

Recently, once again in the field, the men failed to eliminate Stephanie when she ducked a second after the head shot was fired, which caused the bullet to just graze her head.

One fact which became clear, despite all of the bluster, prevarications, and bravado of the captured mercenaries was that not one of them knew who the last shooter was, for whom he worked, or from where he had come. They did say that occasionally, when they were stalking the compound, they would find just a wisp of evidence that someone else might be there, trying to do what they were trying to do, or to make sure they did it.

Chapter Fifteen

Additional Opposition

In the "debriefing session" that was held when everyone was back home, Stephanie asked with a mixture of real anger and sorrow for the young guardswoman who had impersonated her, "Well, what did we learn from this tragedy?" Her sorrow was especially acute, since it was she who had first suggested the idea of a trap!

Leigh responded, "Despite the losses, here is what we know! There has been a mercenary unit stalking the research team. The fact that it was a five man team and each man was given a half million dollars up front, with a promise of another half million upon successful completion of the mission, says there is real money involved. We also know that there is at least one assassin and possibly more, on another team, about which the first team had no knowledge whatsoever. We know that the other team is even more skilled than the first. We know that this other person was so skilled that he or she was able to garrote my guardsman, who was a highly skilled veteran of many years of service. We also know that, despite all of the assets that we had converging on the spot, this person was able to fire three deadly shots and evade my entire team which had been set up for hours to capture the assassins. There are only a very few assassins in the world who can operate successfully at that level of expertise. I would be willing to bet that there are some experts in Virginia, not too far from Washington, who have an active dossier, even if they do not have a picture."

Leigh continued, "The events of today lead me to believe that we have just provided a pretty good reason for those paranoid people in Washington who I talked about earlier, to be even more paranoid! I wouldn't be surprised if we get visitors from back east at any time, if, in fact, they are not already here. At the very least, their attention is going to be peaked! Ethan, I'm going to have to ask if I can use your phone another time."

Somber, Ethan just nodded. It was beginning to sink in, that if he hadn't insisted that Stephanie not go, it would be she who was laid out, ready for transport, and not that unfortunate young woman who had agreed to impersonate her. The more he thought about that, the angrier he became.

Suddenly, he could contain it no longer. "This has got to stop! First, Stephanie is almost killed, then Rachel and her security guard are killed, and now three more of your people, Commander. When is this going to end?"

"The question deserved an answer," thought the commander, but before she could attempt to give one, the phone connection was made.

"Governor, Ethan just asked the question, "When is this all going to stop?' My answer to him is the same as if you had asked the question, which you probably would have in about a minute? This is how I would answer you and him. 'I can't answer your question, but I can tell you that I know my entire battalion of people well, and the deaths of their comrades make them every bit as angry as they have you.' Governor, here is what has transpired since we last spoke." Leigh then gave a synopsis of what they had found out, what they had done, and what had happened.

Stephanie broke into the conversation with the governor when it seemed a good time. "Governor, you asked me to check our findings and we have done so. What we have found and analyzed in all but the most distant test sites, which we have yet to be able to revisit, supports the hypothesis that, despite the time that has elapsed since the earthquake and initial release of toxicity into the ground water, there has been no decrease in the contamination! Normally, given time, the toxic level readings should have gone down, but they have not. On the contrary, not only do the readings show that in almost all sites the percentage of contamination has increased, but also the depth. You will probably remember that our fear of an increase in depth has to do with a possible poisoning of the aquifer. The only conclusion that my team and I have been able to deduce from the data so far is that there is a continuing source of contaminated material being released. We have made some initial progress in studying a process of decontamination, but unless the source of contamination is stopped, that decontamination process has no chance of succeeding."

"Stephanie, did I hear you correctly, that the ground is still being poisoned?"

"Yes, Governor!"

"Thank you, Stephanie. Commander, are you still there?"

"Yes, Governor!"

"I want you to stay put for the next half hour. I am going to make some calls and I will get back to you, understood?"

"Of course, Governor!"

Twenty minutes later the phone came alive again and it was the governor.

"Just a second, Governor, I want to put you on speaker. Is that ok?"

"Yes, it is ok, Commander. By my order, and at the direction of certain people in Washington who, at their request will remain anonymous at this time, I direct you to take as much force as you deem necessary to take over and secure that toxic waste facility. You are ordered to secure all documentation and files. You are further ordered to secure all personnel and place them under arrest and detain them securely. In addition, you are ordered to escort Stephanie and her entire team to the waste facility and turn that place upside down until you find the source of contamination, and then take such measures that are necessary to stop the source of continued contamination. Are there any questions?"

Wide eyed, all of the people present answered in unison, "No, Governor, no questions at all!"

"Good! Commander, get crackin'! I'm tired of fooling around with these people!"

Ray had come into the room a few minutes before, and it was he who was the first to speak. "I presume that was the governor?"

There was a general, consenting nod.

"Commander, that sounded like marchin' orders to me! Well, what do you know? I didn't think the governor had it in her! Stephanie, that sounded like you were included. Seems like you best be putting your stompin' boots on!"

"Mr. Granger, when you're right, you're right!" replied Leigh, "I am going to get the troops ready and this time we are taking the deuce and a half and I am going to have people 'locked and loaded!' Stephanie, how much time do you need?"

"We'll be ready when you are. What would you say it will take your people to be ready?"

"Thirty minutes!"

"Then we will be ready in thirty minutes!"

Chapter Sixteen

Facility Captured

It was a little over an hour later when all of the commander's people and all of Stephanie's remaining people arrived at the front gate of the waste facility. The intimidated security guard challenged the first vehicle, which contained the commander.

"This is private property! You have no jurisdiction here, and I warn you, I saw you coming and called for additional security. Here they come now!"

Two white jeeps with three people each arrived with a screech.

The commander stood up in the humvee with her M16 seemingly casually placed across the top of the windshield.

"I am ordered by the governor of California to take and hold this facility, and take all people who are here into custody. I am ordered to do that with as much force as is necessary."

At a prearranged signal that she gave, guardsmen in the first two trucks pulled up the canvas sides and revealed, among other things, mounted fifty caliber machine guns.

"I need to call the administration!" said the guard.

"I don't think that would be wise, Sir!"

At another signal, there was the loud click, as all the safeties, on all the weapons were disengaged.

The security guard who seemed to be in charge, said "Put 'em down men, there will be another time!"

The white bar barrier was lifted, the security people taken under guard, and the military convoy rolled up the road, a little incongruous against the extensively and expensively landscaped banks that extended up and away from the road. The convoy came to a stop in front of the building that had a large concrete sign which said, "Administration." It was surrounded by flowering plants and, on the sidewalk in front of the sign, an expensively suited man awaited them.

The commander saw immediately that the man was perspiring profusely, and looked like he might faint without much provocation.

"Thank goodness you are here," the suited man said. "These people were here when I came to work this morning. Their leader, in fact all of them that I have seen, look ruthless. I am the plant manager of this firm at present, and as you no doubt know, we have been experiencing some problems of late."

"I would say that is a considerable understatement," responded the commander.

The commander took a portable bull horn from the back seat, pressed the trigger and said, "I would like to speak with the person who has taken control of this facility, as it is evident that the man before me is no longer in control!"

It took a few minutes, but before long, a tall, expensively and elegantly dressed, man appeared on the balcony of the administration building. He was rather handsome, in a severe, narrow faced sort of way.

"Astute of you, Commander Hunnecutt, and my people inform me that the formidable Mrs. Carson is nearby as well. She is a worthy opponent, as are you, Commander, but enough of the pleasantries! You already know that the conglomerate that ran this facility, in its greed for greater profits, used shoddy materials in the construction of its holding ponds. The people who I represent saw the potential and became financial backers of the facilities' expansion and did not discourage the idea that corners could be cut, in order to increase the bottom line profits. My people knew of the earth's inherent instability in this area and had the patience to let nature take its course. As Mrs. Carson has no doubt discovered, the holding ponds and storage tanks continue to leech their poisons into the surrounding farmland and groundwater. At first, these greedy people tried to dissuade Mrs. Carson with political and economic pressure, and then they used more dramatic efforts. It was in my employer's interest, I believe Mrs. Carson's euphemism for them is "conglomerate," to make sure that this land did not return to production, and that is when they had the foresight to find and hire me to act as a countervailing force to that petite juggernaut, Mrs. Carson. It was I who fired those three shots, killing who I mistakenly thought was Mrs. Carson. By the way, my congratulations to the marksman who returned fire at the aqueduct. Had I been a second slower, his bullet would have surely killed me. To my consternation, I found that even I had failed! If conditions were different, I would very much like to meet that young woman, but alas, I will have to forego that pleasure. Now, I am sure I have answered many of your questions, but what you need to know right now is that the ponds and holding tanks have all been rigged to blow at a signal from me. You should also know, Commander, should you be entertaining any wild ideas, that the method that I have designed for the explosions is one that will maximize the continued release of the varied poisons into the groundwater. You also need to know that my people have come from their places of concealment in the foliage along the road and your rear is blocked. It happens to suit my purpose, and because you and Mrs. Carson have been excellent opponents, I will allow you to withdraw, but should you make the mistake of misunderstanding my resolve and decide to open fire, I assure you I have the men in place to eliminate you! Oh, and of course, the charges will then be detonated!"

The commander responded, "We will withdraw for the present, but you may be sure that either I or others will be back!

I hold no illusions to the contrary, Commander!"

Chapter Seventeen

Facility Destroyed

Just as soon as the military convoy withdrew to a safe distance, well beyond the entrance of the facility, a phone call was made to the governor, who told the commander to stay on the line while she made another call. It wasn't ten minutes, until she came back on the line to the commander.

"As we speak, aircraft from the U.S. Naval Air Master Jet Station at Lemoore are being readied for an attack on the waste facility with armor piercing incendiary missiles for the storage tanks, and laser guided incendiary bombs for the ponding basins. Since we want to make sure there is nothing left to be blown up, in any way, by the people you described, we are using veteran pilots who have just returned from deployment at sea, rather than the new pilots who are continually being trained at the station. When I talked to Washington just now and gave them the description you gave me, it did not take them long to identify with whom you talked and the kind of people for whom he worked. You were indeed fortunate to have lost as few of your battalion as you did! Commander, does your command have "laser painting" equipment with you?"

"Yes Governor, like the commercial said, "We don't leave home without it!""

A chuckling governor replied, "Good, because the Navy wants some of your people to "paint the targets" with the lasers so that the various specialized weapons will be delivered to the specific targets, while other targets that do not contain the waste, will be destroyed by more conventional bombs and missiles. Commander, the Navy took pains to tell me that whoever you get to use those lasers need to have stressed to them that they need to be as far as possible away from the targets and still have the lasers work. Your personnel who are tasked with 'painting the tanks' are asked to 'paint' them as close to the top of the tank as possible. The explosive mixture and fusing of the missiles has been redesigned so that the missiles will puncture the tank steel with as little damage to the tank as possible and then the shaped explosive will ignite the incendiary mixture in such a way that the contents of the tank will be consumed by fire, but the force of the explosion will go up through the top of the tank where the missile penetrated, leaving the tank sides and the bottom of the tank intact. The bombs the Navy will be delivering are converted GBU-28 or 'Bunker busters,' so your people just need to 'paint' the center of the holding ponds themselves."

"Apparently after my last conversation with Washington, the authorization was given to the Navy to prepare the weapons. As you can probably tell by the detail, much discussion with the Navy has gone on prior to your call, in a just in case you need us, type discussion. I found out that an explosive expert was flown to NAS Lemoore for a custom designed conversion of the missiles and bombs. He took part of the high explosive out of the bomb casing to eliminate the bomb's depth penetrating power and replaced it with some kind of secret combination of white phosphorus and magnesium, an extremely powerful incendiary. The remaining explosive was reconfigured and refused for the express purpose of igniting the incendiary combination, to not only burn those toxic substances in place, but to scour the containment concrete of the holding ponds without damaging it. Oh, one more thing, Commander, in order to maximize the surprise element by eliminating jet noise, and at the commander of the air base's suggestion, the Navy will circle west from the base, well north of your position, so that the jets will be approaching from the west to take advantage of as much of the low hills as possible. The first wave of jets will pop up just over the hills, fire the weapons at the targets indicated by the lasers, and turn back west, so that their jet noise will not alert the people at the facility until it's too late for them to do anything. Consequently, your people will need to be consistently "painting the targets," as much as possible, from the west. I say consistently because your people won't have the alert by the jet noise either. There will be a second wave of jets just behind the first wave, to make sure all of the targets have been eliminated. These jets will not need the targets illuminated by your people's lasers because the fires will do that for them. The Navy wants to give your people an hour to get in position, and to give the people at the facility a little bit of time to relax their guard!"

"Got it?"

"Got it, Governor, will do!"

It didn't take as long to get the people chosen for the various tasks and on their way with the proper instructions, as it had for the governor to give them.

Once those guardsmen were on the way, the commander turned to the rest of them and said, "There is going to be quite a series of huge explosions and fire balls, which should take care of all of the toxic waste stored at the facility in all of the tanks and ponds, and it may well take care of the people who have taken over the facility as well, but we cannot depend on that! In ten minutes, I want the rest of you dispersed at a safe distance on every road and trail out of that place, so if any of the mercenaries do get out, either before the explosion or after, that we are there to ensure their capture! You have already seen what their leader can do. Don't take any chances! Now get going!"

Stephanie, Ethan, and the research team which remained waited as patiently as they could, knowing that they would just get in the way in this part of the operation, but when the commander had finished, Stephanie spoke up.

"Leigh, we knew that we would just be in the way in the part of the operation you just described, but I wonder two things. First, has anyone thought of alerting the fire service so that they will have assets on site to contain any part of the fire that does not stay where it is desired?"

"Excellent question, Stephanie. I'm going to let you ask it of the governor and she handed Stephanie the special phone."

Stephanie brought the commander up to date with "The answer was no, but she just set the wheels in motion to get the nearest California Forest Service Fire Department assets here fast, with others coming. The first units should be here about the time the jets arrive!"

"What's the second question, Stephanie?"

"My team has been rapidly becoming experts on toxic waste, and one thing is for sure. They are the closest 'experts' around! Would you like us to come in and assess the extent of neutralization, just as soon as you and the fire service say it's safe, of course?"

"Another excellent question, Stephanie, and my answer is, 'yes, and thank you, as long as you abide by the second part of what you asked me!' I am positive that the governor would be, shall we say displeased with me, if I let anything happen to you or your team at this stage. Now, what do you say if we find a little more distant, protected location to await the coming events?"

In a surprisingly short time, and without any preceding jet engine noise, there was a sustained series of almost simultaneous ear splitting explosions, followed by a long sustained succession of tremendous balls of fire and black roiling smoke and flame that climbed thousands of feet into the sky. There seemed to be a miniscule lull in the explosions, only to be followed by more explosions, produced by the second wave of aircraft. These were as loud as, or even louder than, the first set, so much so that the onlookers could only point in mute amazement. Soon there was an oily ash found settling downwind for miles.

Stephanie's forethought of the fire service enabled them to be on hand in a short amount of time. Due of their expertise, and being aided by the absence of the heavy winds that sometimes plagued the area, the forest service was able to bring the collateral fire damage under control.

When Stephanie and her team were permitted into the remains of the facility, and even though they had heard the explosions and seen the fire and smoke, they were still surprised at the amount of controlled explosive force. All of the neatly landscaped yards and the spotless buildings they had seen just minutes before were a thing of the past. However, the white storage tanks looked a little like someone had taken a giant can opener to the tops, exposing the interior, while the concrete storage ponds were empty, save for the ash that was settling on them. Gone were, apparently all, of the stored toxic compounds that had been stored at the vast facility. The initial facility has been much smaller, but since the expansion of the compound the amount of material that could be stored there had grown to tremendous volume.

The governor had ordered that Stephanie and her team find the source of the leakage, but Stephanie could see that until the debris was cleaned, that would not be possible.

During the complete and careful sweep of the whole compound, the guardsmen came across a large underground vault. The commander was called to the scene, where her guardsmen discovered, and the commander secured, a large quantity of files which had been locked in a large bank size walk in safe.

The commander called for Stephanie. Once Stephanie had been escorted to the vault, the commander said, "It's going to take some time for us to get the site safe for you to study, but I thought you and your team might use the time to advantage by studying these files."

Stephanie's reply was tinged with excitement, "These files might contain information that could shorten our search by days or more! Based on what 'the man' said, they knew where the leaks were and probably what poisons and in what quantities they had been stored!"

Chapter Eighteen

Enemy Within

It had taken some time to control the fire and secure the area, and then to have Stephanie's team do their research, but in a week, the whole combined team of National Guard and researchers returned to Ethan and Stephanie's ranch, exhausted, extremely dirty, but ebullient in a tired sort of way, satisfied that a good job had been done. On the way home, Stephanie invited Leigh to use their second shower and Leigh at first refused, saying she should be with her people, but with a little nudging, she gratefully agreed to accept Stephanie's hospitality.

In turn, Ethan invited Stephanie to use the master bathroom shower first, and she hadn't needed any nudging to accept. Refreshed, she got out of Ethan's way, and in turn, he didn't lose any time submitting his body to the cleansing spray. Since he was last, he indulged himself with a thorough muscle mending water massage, so that, when he emerged, it was probably thirty minutes since the time he entered. Combed, shaved, and dressed in a casual set of slacks and shirt, he drifted down toward the living room. He was on the upper landing, when for some reason, his personal alarm bells started ringing and he stopped cold!

A voice called to him, "Well, the master emerges. Come on down and join the party, Ethan!"

Seated in the living room was Stephanie in her robe.

"That's what must have set me off, Ethan thought to himself, "Stephanie never comes downstairs in her robe!"

Beside Stephanie, in another of her robes, was Leigh, who looked as though she had resisted and had been banged up a bit. Ray lay on the sofa, and he didn't look good at all. There was a cloth on his head with a quantity of blood seeping from it. Seated opposite to them was 'the man' who the commander had described to the governor, the man who she had seen on the administration building's veranda. Seemingly placed haphazardly on his lap, was an automatic pistol with a silencer attached to the muzzle. Unlike those pistols sometimes seen in the movies, this one did not have a large multi round cartridge magazine. The man, being a true professional, the pistol contained only the standard magazine. At his side, propped against the arm of the chair, was evidently one of those sniper rifles that the commander had described.

"Well, of all the nerve," Ethan said under his breath when he saw that the man was wearing one of the new suits which Stephanie had encouraged him to buy, once she was more comfortable in the role of being his wife, and had evaluated his wardrobe. In the milliseconds that it took him to remember the evaluation of his dress wardrobe that led to new purchases, he started down the stairs.

The man, who had followed Ethan's eyes, said "Not exactly my style and it's a trifle small, but what I had been wearing was beyond saving. I was just about to say to the commander that I congratulate her on her rapid response, and the fact that as far as I know right now, I am the only one who evaded her net. I must be losing my edge. First I didn't succeed in killing your wife, and then I misjudged the commander. It must be time for me to retire, and you all are going to help me do just that. Due to your activities, the airports will be closed to me, and both Mexico and Canada are much too far away, so that leaves the coast. Ethan, you are going to call this number. You will probably recognize it, since I got it from the rolodex that I am guessing was your father's, since you don't look to me like a rolodex type guy. It is the number of a charter boat service, that, according to your father's notation, had given him satisfaction. Please say that you want to rent a large fishing boat for a two day charter, that you and some friends will be arriving late this evening and will want to set out for an evening on the water, and would he please stock provisions for five."

At the mention of his father, the color on Ethan's neck started flushing enough for the armed man to notice, just as Ethan was beginning to shift his weight in preparation for attack.

"Ethan, I can see you are getting angry, and angry people sometimes make bad decisions. Please settle down. I don't want you to do anything foolish. If you're thinking that I killed your father, I didn't. Although I don't know it for a fact, I think it was one or more of those slugs who you have in custody, under guard, with the commander's military police. That particular action took place before the people that I represent got uncomfortable enough with the local company's actions to arrange for me and my team to be here. I suppose you could say I am their "problem solver!"

"Ethan will you please make that call?"

Ethan did as he was told, but something told him to embellish his report when he hung up. With a shudder that he tried to suppress, he couldn't help thinking that there was a lot of water in, and outside, of Morro Bay, water that could hide a lot of bodies for a long time.

"Arturo said that his boat cannot be ready in time because he is having the bottom cleaned, but he was pretty sure he can get a friend's boat, which is not as nice or as large as his, but will do for our purpose. He said he will call me in about an hour to verify that he has it ready for us."

"Stephanie, why don't you see to the frisky gentleman who I presume is your father, given the common facial features I see. Why don't you get some ice and try to stop the bleeding? When I came to the door, impersonating one of your early returning research team, he invited me in to clean up. I don't know what led him to suspect me, but before I had even gotten into the room, he stopped me, and I had to clip him twice, in order for him to stay down!"

Just as Stephanie rose to go get the ice, Ethan did as he was told, and had settled in his seat just a bit, when the doorbell rang.

"Easy does it folks. Ethan, please see who it is and what they want, and then get rid of them as soon as possible!"

Ethan answered the door and found Alex there. Before they had left for the visit to the waste facility, Ethan had gone to the pump house and unlocked it. Ethan had told Alex where they were going and that it might be awhile before they got back. He added that he was going to trust Alex not to run, and to look after the place. Ethan also took the time to tell Alex that, although they did not have time now to go into it, he wanted to talk to him about the money he had lost. Ethan was glad he had decided to do that, because after he had told Alex, the man had choked up and said that Mr. Ethan could trust him to do what he asked.

"Excuse me, Mr. Ethan, I just wanted you to see I was still here!" said Alex.

"Oh Alex, it is good to see you. Of course you are still here. It is tomorrow that I want you to go to town. Will you please take these keys and bring the car that is in the garage to the front door. I think that some, or all of us, will be leaving for a little relaxation after all the events of the last few days and I would like for you to drive us! Thank you for reminding me that you are still here, and for getting the car!"

"Sure Mr. Ethan, anything you say!"

Alex was on the way to the garage to get the car, when he stopped in his tracks to think!

"What the…Mr. Ethan didn't tell me that he wanted me to go to town, and he knows I lost my license, because of the DUI I got awhile back. In fact, he had said he was peeved at me because that meant I couldn't do any work that required driving, and especially that I couldn't do any that required me to drive to town. So why did he ask me to bring the good car around? Come to think of it, he knows that I can't go to town, as part of my punishment. So why was he telling me to bring a car around? That whole conversation sounded like something wasn't quite right! I think I'm going to stroll over to those military people and tell them. I don't know exactly why, but it just doesn't sound right!" Once he told them, he felt better, and went back toward the garage to get the car. Just in case he was making a "mountain out of a mole hill," he was going to be sure he did as he was asked.

Lieutenant Lyle Krough, the second in command to Leigh Hunnecutt had been convinced by Alex's tale that something wasn't right. Convinced by the foreman that something was amiss, he had Alex stopped before he had gone thirty feet. After rapid, but unobtrusive and undetected search of the outside of the house and an internal search by infrared scan, a man was revealed who appeared to be holding something that looked a lot like a gun, someone who was lying prone with a hot spot on his head, and three people seated closely together. It was obvious that an assault on the home would result in multiple casualties, as would an assault on the car, if it were allowed to approach the house in a conventional way. Lieutenant Krough was a small, wiry officer, known for his perhaps too Prussian attitude, and thus was not as popular with the rank in file, as was the commander.

Popular or not, his quick thinking came up with a possible plan. Since Alex had said that the participants in the house might be planning some evening's diversion, it occurred to the lieutenant that embroidery on that theme might provide an opportunity to separate the armed man from the "friendlies." Lieutenant Krough had Sergeant Jack coordinate with the cook, who got a hastily prepared façade of a celebration on track, and he had a word with the leader of the unit's musical section. Then there was the preparation of Alex to play his role in the farce, designed to get the assault unit unobtrusively between the two sections of the party as they emerged from the house. The first direction to Alex was to make sure he parked the car far enough from the front door so that, not only the band could "surprise" the emerging party from each side with enough levity as to not alarm the armed man into a defensive posture, but in addition, the cooks would have room to set up the table beyond the band. Another two man team, led by Sergeant Jack, was stationed behind a table clothed table, with the cloth tethered to the ground so that an errant breeze would not reveal their presence.

Interspersed within the band were to be the "action squad," whose task was to do one of two things, depending upon the developing situation, neutralize the threat by either bringing him to the ground, or if necessary, and without unnecessary collateral damage, take him out. Lyle briefly considered trying to protect the others from the man, but that multiplied the focus, too many people to protect within too short a time frame.

Lyle Krough's job was to sidle up to the commander and put his arm around her shoulder just as soon as Alex led them from the house and to start the singing, "They are Jolly Good People" with the lyrics changed a bit to fit the situation. He was going to pretend to be just a bit tipsy, and he hoped that, since the commander knew he was a teetotaler, that it would alert her to expect the unexpected. Other specifically assigned people were to do essentially the same with each friendly member who was now within the compound. The largest man in the whole unit, was Franklyn, who easily topped six feet, five inches, and just as easily, carried a three hundred pound frame. His gentle face belied his physical strength. His assigned task was to put his arm around the armed man and mimic what the other special team members had been assigned.

This plan had been hastily designed, and Lyle knew that at least a hundred things could go wrong, but even if everything else went wrong, he was hoping that Franklyn's part would go right!

The "action squad" was concealed, the table and cloth were in place, and the show of a party was being shuttled rapidly into place. It was time for Alex to make a sound as if he had trouble starting the car, then start it, and move into place. If asked, his excuse was to be that the car hadn't been used lately, and that, at least, was true.

Alex was at the door, and went into his little speech.

"Mr. Ethan, the car is ready," he improvised a bit. "I had a little trouble starting it. It hasn't been driven much lately."

Ethan responded to Alex at a signal from the armed man, "Ok, Alex, just leave the keys in it. I've decided to drive."

Alex was panicked! This wasn't according to the plan! He got a signal from Lyle to keep the conversation going, so he improvised again. "Mr. Ethan, there are some folks out here who heard that you and the missus might be leaving for a bit, and they wanted to be sure and say goodbye proper. They're signaling me to ask you, Miz' Stephanie, Mr. Ray, and the commander, all out for just a bit, if you please?"

Lyle gave Alex the thumbs up and waited.

In a few minutes, as if they had to get ready, out they came, and the plan went into action. A quick movement in the armed man's peripheral vision caused him to slip his hand into the pocket of Ethan's jacket, which he was wearing, but when the music started, muscles relaxed, and at the same time, the actors took their places.

The band began to play, and a "tipsy" lieutenant started the singing and the others joined in. Before the words of the chorus could be sung, the curtain had come down on the little play, with cheers by all, all except one. The man, who was the objective of the exercise, was literally pinned on the ground, gasping for breath, while the gentle giant, who had a little cut and some bruised ribs, sat on him, with a smile from ear to ear!

The quickly planned farce party, with what food the unit's cooks could muster on almost a minute's notice, became a real one, when Stephanie added what she could from their pantry, and that was combined with Ethan's expressly organized barbequed tri-tip steak and Alex's famous baked beans. The party became a real wingding!

Later that night, after Leigh had phoned the governor and given her the most recent update, and had time to revive a bit from her roughing up, she and Ray got a chance to talk about old movies and one of their favorite character actors, and in which version of a particular classic movie, "the Duke" had played with her grandfather. Ray, an avid classic movie buff was ecstatic when he heard that Leigh had inherited movie prints of all of her grandfather's movies!

The next morning, the "slugs" were shackled to the floor of one of the National Guard deuce and a half trucks, surrounded by armed guards, who had orders to shoot if necessary.

In another deuce and a half, "the man" was shackled, hand and foot, with even a heavy leather collar hastily fashioned and fastened to the floor with a hefty chain, but only after he had been "thoroughly" searched by men who knew their business. A trio of armed men, plus Franklyn, were assigned to ride with him, in order to keep eyes on him at all times.

Behind the two prisoner vehicles was the guard of honor for the three guardsmen who had fallen "into the trap." Events had escalated so quickly that another honor guard had not been able to be ordered from Fairfield, so Ethan had seen to it that a greater portion of their walk-in-refrigerator in the barn had been made ready and the three casualties had been properly coffined and flag-covered there, until a proper honor guard could take them home.

After the last loss, the honor guard, tasked with taking the fallen guardsman home, had brought with them a small supply of coffins, should there be additional need. Unfortunately, there had been, and three of their number filled half of the coffins that had been provided!

The column, with Leigh in the lead humvee, and the field promoted, Lyle, beside her, the battalion of National Guard military police started down the hill and around "Ear Rock" on the long trek back to Fairfield.

Stephanie couldn't help remarking, as she had seemingly a life time ago, but in reality just a couple of months ago, that if Interstate 5 hadn't been a ghost of its former self, their journey would have been a lot more rapid. When the last vehicle went under the wrought iron three hill silhouette, she turned to the team, squared her shoulders, and said, "As the governor said not so long ago, 'Let's get crackin'!' We've got a ton of work to do!"

As if in one voice, the team answered, "She's baaack!" and all of them, Stephanie included, broke out laughing, the tension of the last few weeks melting away with the laughter!

Chapter Nineteen

A Startling Speculation

The next morning, at about eight o'clock, following a meeting with the research team, Stephanie was still in the big tent, when, out of the blue, she blurted out something that apparently had been processing in her fertile mind, without her full awareness. "Why had the conglomerate bought out the facility, if, after such a little while, it was willing to have its "problem solver" blow it up, and lose the entire investment? That doesn't make sense! Think about it. The facility expanded, got into trouble financially, and then the conglomerate took a controlling interest and, at least for a while, let the facility operate at increased capacity. Then the earthquake occurred, caused enough damage to create a massive underground release, but rather than fix the leak, the conglomerate let the facility continue to operate as if there was no leak. They had to realize there was a leak long before the poisoning of the surrounding area, long before my research, for no other reason than that the levels in the ponds would have been going down. The commander said that Washington thought it might be eco-terrorism. What if, rather than eco-terrorism, the same original motive of the company was still at work, greed, just on a much larger scale? It was thought that 'the man' might be a 'terrorist.' If he were a terrorist, he could have taken out a lot of people when the commander's unit rolled into the facility, yet he let it go. He certainly had time, while he was here, to 'take a lot of us out,' but he didn't. Why? Perhaps his earlier failed attempt on me was just another try at slowing our research by the conglomerate?"

Although her outburst had been addressed at no one in particular, in an instant she had captured the attention of those who had heard and, as if mesmerized, the members of the team, who had already started the process of the research designated for the day, were drawn from their work stations toward her.

"Team, try this on for size," Stephanie continued, "The conglomerate bought the facility, not to eventually plan to release the toxins in a terrorist attack, but to operate it as a test facility! They needed a constant and varied supply of toxic poisons because they were thinking 'light-years' ahead of me. They knew that there are regular oil spills, and it would be just a matter of time before there would be regular toxic waste spills.

What if they were using the facility as a research laboratory to develop a marketable series of products with the specific purpose of having a ready supply of proven 'clean- up' products for a whole range of toxic wastes? With a monopoly on that market, they could write their own price tag. Look at some of the recent oil spills. How much was spent on cleanup efforts? The earthquake and then my research were bothersome, because they were nearing completion of their research and product production. They needed to slow us down, so the 'slugs' were specifically tasked to continue to harass and sidetrack us, but the conglomerate brought in their 'problem-solver,' for a 'just in case' scenario.

We know they had weapons and support enough to mount a real attack on our facility. When we went to the waste facility, 'the man's' team had either just finished laying charges or almost laying charges. Why? Because their research and product production were, for all intents and purposes, complete, and they had to 'get rid of any embarrassing evidence' that might come out, once they began to market their new line of 'clean-up' technologies. Once their product line hit the shelves, it would be subject to scrutiny and possible lawsuit if anyone could find evidence of how the products had been produced."

"Team, can anyone see any holes in the analysis? I know it's a combination of supposition and conjecture, but does it omit any evidence which we know might make it just a 'waking nightmare?'"

Several of the team started a list of the parts of Stephanie's analysis on a lab white board and started analyzing Stephanie's epiphany. They wanted to see if any of the "connected dots" of Stephanie's outburst would start forming a pattern that would support Stephanie's tentative hypothesis. Before long, they had to conclude that they didn't know if it was an accurate assessment, but most of the major components, and a lot of the minor ones, formed, at least one possible interpretation. Whether it was, in reality, the true one, they did not yet have enough data to prove conclusively.

Since, once again, the scope of this new possibility was beyond the research team's mandate through the university, but seemed to be a part of the governor's mandate, it was Stephanie's turn to call the governor, using the number that Leigh had left, "just in case!"

The case was laid out for the governor, who rather than take notes, turned on a tape-recorder. Upon the completion of the recitation of Stephanie's scenario, the governor let out a small gasp, and said, "I knew there was more to it, but I hadn't put my finger on it! Stephanie, what you have suggested is over my head. I'm going to have to call Washington. Is it ok to use your name when I tell this?"

"Sure, Governor, just remember it may be a paranoid delusion, but it holds together with what we know of the situation. Oh, one more thing, Governor, I am tired of calling 'the man,' 'the man.' Did anyone actually find out who he really was?"

The governor responded, "I'll ask about the name as well. Maybe they will even tell me! I suppose you know that, if just a little of this is proved accurate, we will have some pretty deep pockets from which to draw to cover the cleanup."

"I suppose you are right, Governor. I can honestly say we hadn't thought of that!"

"Stephanie, you and your team are priceless! I'll get back to you with what I find out!"

Chapter Twenty

Solution Sleuthing

Sufficiently recovered, and seeing that Stephanie was back and 'goin' great guns,' Stephanie's father, Ray, said that he had been away from his farm and congregation too long and needed to get back home. Both Ethan and Stephanie objected because they had gotten used to Ray being there with them, but Ethan could see the logic in his father-in-law's rationale, at least about his needing to get back to his farm.

Nothing was heard from the governor for a while, but that didn't keep the team from working.

Based on the possibility that Stephanie was right, a re-tasked sub group of the team was made. The premise of that sub-team was, whether or not Stephanie was right, and clean up products had been made, or if not made, could be made, what was the method by which they might be applied to the land here in the western Central Valley where the damage had been done?

First on their list was the possible method that Stephanie had proposed in her initial work: a process of washing the soil, then a cleansing of the wash water, and then a rewashing, until the soil was clean. Although that was a theoretically possible process, the actual method of accomplishing it needed to be worked out in an actual working method.

Other teams worked on other possible ways of decontaminating the soil, a bio-friendly method of powering whatever process might be decided upon, and other methods of a more direct cleansing, using already developed techniques, but a reapplication of them. Additionally, the lab team was still working on decontamination materials in case the proposed clean up products were faulty or inapplicable, or did not exist.

All of Stephanie's ideas were tested, natural or man-made, as well as many more. Ground penetrating radar imaging and sound impact resonance imaging were considered for finding existing underground water channels.

Reverse osmosis filtering, semi-permeable membrane piping, and horizontal drilling were just some of the ideas examined for filtering underground water. Methods for cleansing the soil included washing the soil and then washing the water, bio-technologies of planting a series of crops designed to leach out a series of identified chemicals, as well as, using wicking ponds to leach out certain contaminates.

All were examined for feasibility, cost to return, and length of implementation to satisfactory end result. A small box was even constructed with contaminated soil and filled part way with water to test the "wick-out" theory. When at all possible, actual tests were made to demonstrate the theories.

About a week after Stephanie's call to the governor, the team received a call from the "hazard materials" unit that had been sent in to clean up what was left of the waste facility. The site was ready for Stephanie's team to return and complete their inspection, to find and determine the source of the leak or leaks, and whether or not they were actually nature made by the earthquake or deliberate weaknesses that were designed to fail. The work at the compound was put on hold and the team traveled to complete what the governor had asked them to do.

What they found was both reassuring and frightening! Despite the explosions created by the bombing, the fractures in the original tanks and holding ponds appeared consistent with what had been caused by the earthquake, rather than purposely built in flaws.

What was frightening was three fold. First, the newer tanks that had been built after the expansion of the waste facility were just barely within specifications, with no margin of safety. Second, the sheer number of tanks and ponds that had failed was disconcerting. Third, from all that could be seen, no attempt to repair the failed tanks or ponds after the earthquake had ever been attempted!

In short, nothing the team found in the days they spent examining the cleaned up facility contradicted what Stephanie had theorized. The team returned, both reassured that they might be on the right track, but somber at the callousness of purpose of what they had found.

Chapter Twenty-one

Witness Protection

A few days after Stephanie and the team returned to the compound, the governor called. "Stephanie, as you can probably tell, Washington was not quick to answer your questions, even though they were communicated by me! I've got to tell you that made me more than a little impatient, and I started throwing a little muscle of my own around! I think one of the reasons I was being given the "I'll get back to you!" treatment, was that certain people were so glad that it wasn't eco-terrorism, that they immediately lost interest! I started making some progress when I pointed out that, although it might not have been eco-terrorism, much the same economic destruction had taken place. I've found that if there is a way for me to play the money card, I can get certain influential people interested. Right now, while no one is saying you are right, there are the beginnings of international investigations and damage suits being prepared, with the State of California being a major complainant, not seeking hundreds of millions, but billions of dollars in damages. Therefore, I think it safe to say, that even if it turns out that you weren't completely right, the difference is hardly worth mentioning. Don't be surprised, if you and members of your team get subpoenas to deliver testimony. By the way, if there are any travel or expense costs involved, the state will pick up the tab. Oh, you asked about 'the man.' It is interesting that you should ask, because when he left the California National Guard custody, he vanished, and the Feds aren't saying 'boo,' about it. So once again, I will be sending the National Guard to protect you and your team. When she was told, Leigh Hunnecutt requested the assignment and I concurred, so she and the Guard unit are already coming your way. As far as 'the man's' name, no one, as far as I have been able to find out, actually knows his real name. He is like that assassin a few years back named 'Carlos.' No one knew his name. He was just given one for convenience. Our man's name is 'Henri,' since some people say he 'looks' French, and some say he was heard to speak French. Given our modern identification technologies, that identification seems woefully inadequate."

"Thank you for the update, Governor! Now, let me give you one." Stephanie related what they had found at the site, as well as, an overview of the progress they had made in the compound.

Chapter Twenty-two

Protection Arrives Again

It wasn't much more than an hour later that the National Guard Military Police from Fairfield once again rolled under the wrought iron arch and belched black exhaust as they snaked up the hill and around "'Ear Rock." "The governor hadn't been fooling,' Stephanie thought. 'They must have started over five hours ago!" A now familiar series of events took place, with the drivers rolling the trucks into position and the Guardsmen establishing a perimeter. What with everything that had been happening, the security lights that Ethan had his ranch hands erect had never been taken down, so the generator was turned on and the lights checked, and then shut off until needed later.

Once the guard had been set, Leigh came over to the house. It hadn't been many days, but she appeared recovered with her bruises gone, or at least well-camouflaged. Even considering the reason for her return trip, a happy reunion was had by all. She was now considered part of the family and was treated as such. The governor had briefed her on the salient points of the necessity for the Guard's return trip.

Now Stephanie had an opportunity to fill her in on what they suspected had occurred, which, if not all exactly true, according to the governor, reported Stephanie, the difference between speculation and fact was hardly worth mentioning. Once again, Leigh was impressed with Stephanie's analytical mind and her ability to take seemingly disparate elements and put them together to form a whole picture.

A knock at the door and Ethan's answer, presented Alex, hat in hand.

"Mr. Ethan, I just wanted to say my hellos to the commander, and tell you that the guard appears to be set and the lights and generator checked. The team, once they knew that the commander was here, wanted to say hello and thank you for coming. Miz' Stephanie, they would like to see you in the big tent when you have an opportunity. Some of them think they have something you would like to see."

When Alex had left, Ethan could tell there was a question in the commander's eyes about Alex.

Ethan said simply, "Alex had been duped, then essentially blackmailed. He was so helpful in helping free us, how could we then press charges? He was so grateful when we told him, he almost cried."

"Ethan, you are an even bigger man than you appear!" stated the commander.

Ethan almost said, "Aw shucks, Ma'am, weren't nothin!" and the blush at his neck signaled it for him.

Stephanie, seeing his embarrassment, came to his rescue, "Why don't we go down to the big tent?"

Chapter Twenty-three

Sleuth Success

The team was excited, and all of them started talking at once when Stephanie, Ethan, and Leigh came through the tent flap opening.

"Whoa, one at a time," Stephanie laughed.

The members looked at each other and decided who should go first.

"Ok, they seem to want us to go first, so please come this way," Helen and Jasper said, and they led the group out of the tent to a small grove of trees that seemed to thrive without being watered, since it was evidently beyond the automatic underground sprinkler system that kept the front yard green.

"You will see that this grove appears to thrive, although it is not being watered. So, since this was a handy place, we decided to use it for some non-invasive tests." They produced the ground–imaging radar and the small sound-impact resonance unit. In a few minutes, they had imaging data that clearly showed an underground channel that was bringing a small, but sufficient, amount of water to irrigate the whole grove.

"Do you understand what this means?" Not waiting for an answer, they answered their own question. "With these tools, we can locate natural watering sub-soil channels, if of course, they are not too deep!"

"Well done!" Stephanie could tell that Ethan and Leigh hadn't grasped the import of this discovery yet. "What Helen and Jasper have just demonstrated is a way to track natural underground watering systems, so that, when we have the correct decontaminating agents, we can put them directly into the sub-soil irrigation systems, rather than just watering an entire plot with the water to decontaminate it. This will save us precious time and avoid waste of decontaminate."

Helen and Jasper were once more proud of Stephanie for having seen the importance of their discovery.

"Again, well done! Let's go back and see what the others have for us!"

When they returned to the tent, the next two to present, Ellen and James, showed Stephanie a quantity of the oily ash residue that they had collected from the site when the team had gone back to assess the waste facility before it had been cleaned. A computer print out analysis showed that even the ash had been a mixture of nasty toxic chemicals, leaving no doubt that it was residue from the toxic waste site. The next print out showed a succession of applied reagents. After an application of each reagent, one set of chemicals was neutralized. Much like the application of chemicals in a swimming pool, after each application, a different less toxic reading resulted. After several such steps, the computer analysis demonstrated an absence of toxic readings, with a PH within acceptable norms.

"Another home run! Way to go Ellen and James!" Stephanie effused.

Stephanie was really getting excited at the findings, which were validating the team's hard work, and they all started to almost glow with her praise.

The next two, Claudia and Leroy, began. "What we have for you is a model of a delivery system. If you will come this way, we can demonstrate!" A small Plexiglas box, almost like a large ant farm, held a series of devices. The first device was a miniature of what looked very much like an irrigation pump on the surface. Beside it was a miniature well drilling system, although the pipe, instead of going straight down, went down a few inches and then curved horizontally, so that the pipe was horizontal to the surface, but beneath the soil. There were hash marks on the box that indicated that the marks represented feet. Outside the box was a section of pipe similar to what was within the box. There was a control box with a series of switches. The first switch made the drill apparatus operate, and the drill could be seen advancing, first down, and curving to move horizontally. The second switch made a minute change in the look of the underground pipe. Then it was turned off. One of the team demonstrated what happened inside the box with a separate, larger piece of pipe that was outside the box.

Longitudinal slots appeared in what was evidently an outer pipe, with a kind of filter material covering the slots inside the pipe. The third switch, when activated, first pumped water from a small reservoir outside the box, down the pipe and into the soil. When the fourth switch was flipped, the water flow was reversed and the water in the soil was drawn into the pipe, through the filter material, up to the surface, and through a reverse osmosis filtering system and into another reservoir.

"It's wonderful! Does it really work on a large scale?" Stephanie asked.

"We have tried it in a six by six box, and it appears to," they replied. "Of course, the only way to tell is to build the full scale system and see!"

"Stella and Tom, how did the wick-out pond work?"

"As you might imagine, using a natural wicking out process is slower than direct pumping, but we have seen some progress in leaching some toxic materials to the surface with water containing some reagents. We then piped the water through a series of three of the same model of reverse osmosis filter that Claudia and Leroy used in their experiment, and the data shows significant reduction in toxicity.

"Team, I am tremendously impressed! You all have done exceptionally! When we put these individual pieces together, I think, for the first time, we will have a system that has a real chance at solving the problem! You deserve a standing ovation, and I am giving you one here and now!"

Stephanie, Ethan, and Leigh clapped for a long while, and the team reddened just a bit in the praise.

Once back to the house, both Leigh and Ethan turned to Stephanie and said, almost in unison, "Since I don't have a clue what I just clapped for, will you enlighten me!"

Stephanie laughed, "You're not ignorant. It's just that we have been working together on the complex problem for a while and we understand all the subtext that wasn't there for you."

"Since the toxic chemicals were introduced into the ground water and carried by it, and since we can't see those underground mini-streams, we have to be able 'to see' those streams if we are going to use them to carry the decontaminants. That is what the first demonstration was for, a way to detect the underground mini-streams and use them instead of more wasteful conventional watering. The second demonstration showed that no one 'dose' of decontaminate would be sufficient to neutralize the toxins, but there is a series of 'doses' that will neutralize it. The third demonstration showed that there is an effective way to take the water into the soil, bring contaminated water to the surface, neutralize it, re-inject it, and do it again, again, and again, in a cost effective way. The whole process will have to be repeated many times, but since we can locate the natural underground waterways, the number of times will be much reduced. Of course, we will have to build a full scale model and test it, but now we know what to build, and can find a place to test it! What you just saw, I believe, made the entire process of what we have gone through, including the cost to the university, an investment that will be worth many times its cost!"

It was plain that Ethan was a bit under impressed with what he had seen, when he said, "Now that you have explained what we saw, it seems to me you speculated along those very lines in your original research. What we saw is a small scale version of what you proposed. Isn't that true?"

"I hadn't thought of it that way, but I guess that's true!" A now all too familiar blush, as far as Stephanie was concerned, returned to her cheeks.

"I thought so," said Ethan. "She's a genius, but so willing to recognize the talents of others that she forgets that it was she who thought of it all in the first place!"

"That, my dear sir, is one of the many reasons that I am so fond of your wife," Leigh responded.

"Oh, stop, you two!" said Stephanie, still blushing.

Chapter Twenty-four

Show & Tell

With the progress that had been made in the big tent, it was definitely time to bring the university up to speed, so a call was made to the chancellor. After being given a quick update on recent progress, it was decided that the chancellor, Professor Daniels, and Professor Jacob Lackland of the science department at the University of California, Davis would all make room in their schedules the next day for a first hand complete update and demonstration. The governor's office had kept the chancellor's office informed of the major events, but only in general detail for security reasons.

The chancellor had driven down to Ethan's place once before that summer and knew the kind of time that it would take, given the condition of the road. It was decided to charter a helicopter, in order to cut down the travel time. So the threesome from the university arrived in less than half the time it would have taken by car. The chancellor made a mental note that it really was time to put some pressure on the governor to get the once vital transportation artery that Interstate 5 had been, back to its pre-earthquake capability. After all, the university's enrollment had decreased, due to the increased difficulty of getting there from the Central Valley and points south.

Ethan, the ranch hands, and the team pulled out all the stops in preparation for the visit. A barbeque luncheon was prepared and the big tent was set for the demonstrations, with pictures of the toxic waste site before and after placed on one table. Computer slide shows demonstrated the accumulated research, to date, on another.

While in route, the chancellor decided that it might be enlightening to see what was left of the waste facility, so he had the pilot extend the flight just a bit and circle what was left of the waste facility site, before arriving at Ethan's and Stephanie's ranch.

Leigh didn't want to be the poor sister in this whole event, so she had an honor guard spruce up for a review, but at the same time, she was keenly aware of her primary reason for being there. Therefore, she doubled the perimeter guard and didn't mince any words as to what would happen to any guardsman, if he permitted a threat to Stephanie, the team, or the arriving visitors in getting through.

Ethan had Alex signal the helicopter to land down wind and down at the bottom of a small rise, so that the rotor wash wouldn't blow everything that had been prepared to smithereens. Before the chancellor and the other two men got out, the pilot told them that he would stay and tie the ship down, just in case, and be up as soon as he finished.

It was just a bit of a hike for the three men to get up to the house, and they were just a bit out of breath when they got there.

Stephanie and Ethan could tell that they were pleased at the effort that had been made in preparation for their visit. Stephanie had consulted with the team to see if they concurred with her agenda for the visit. They agreed that probably the first order of business would be to bring the visitors up to date in the house, then take them to the big tent for the demonstrations, and then end up with the luncheon.

In the living room of the big house, with cool drinks in hand, the chancellor, Professor Daniels, and Professor Lackland were brought up to date with the research that had been conducted in the field, the casualties that had been incurred, the sequence of events at the waste facility, the findings that had been made there, the suppositions that had been made, and finally, the advances that had been made, once the threat had been removed. As each event was detailed, the amazement on the three faces became successively more evident.

"I don't know if I said it or someone else, Mrs. Carson, but you never disappoint! Wow, what a tale!" complimented the chancellor.

Professor Daniels and Professor Lackland echoed the same sentiments.

"Now, how about we go see those demonstrations you mentioned," the chancellor said.

"Ok, let's go. The team is dying, scratch that, anxious, to show off!" Stephanie corrected herself in mid-sentence.

The whole group made its' way slowly to the big tent in consideration of Professor Jacob Lackland, who was moving rather slowly and carefully. This was his first real venture into the field after being released from the doctor's care. The internal injuries that he had received when the shooter had missed Stephanie and hit him, were mostly healed, but his arm was still in a soft cast and a sling.

One after another, the demonstrations were made, and the researchers who had made the advances were allowed to explain them and answer questions.

On purpose, Stephanie stood in the background, and thought "This is their show, they have earned it, and they can carry the ball!"

Suitably impressed, the chancellor and the two science professors made effusive complimentary remarks to each member of the team.

When Ethan sensed those questions and compliments abating, he said, "Let's eat!"

Chapter Twenty-five

Enemy Reappears

No one argued with him, so he led the way to the luncheon tables that had been prepared.

When all had eaten all they could eat, and quite probably more than they should have eaten, the chancellor said,

"Stephanie, a special well done is due you and your team, and when the three of us figure out what that might be, we will let you know. Until that time, keep up the good work, and with that, we must get back. Speaking of that, where is our pilot? In the excitement, I confess I forgot all about him!"

"Here I am, Chancellor!"

An all too familiar figure of a man strode up to the table, with an automatic weapon at the ready!

"Henri!" Stephanie breathed.

"Not my name of course, but it will do for now!"

"How did you get here," the chancellor asked, more than a little upset by the sight of the weapon.

"Your university phone system is pretty easy to tap, Chancellor!"

"What can you possibly want here now?" Stephanie asked.

"That is a surprisingly good question, Mrs. Carson, but I guess I shouldn't be surprised at your ability to ask good questions, should I? The last time I was here, I said that I ought to retire, and that is exactly what I plan to do, after I take care of some unfinished business. The people I work for don't pay for failure. In fact, they reward it rather severely! I have amassed sufficient money for me to live an extremely comfortable life, if I am allowed to do that. If I do not properly conclude my last contract, I am sure my employers will see that my retirement is literally short lived. Nothing can be salvaged of the work at the waste site, but if the major witnesses slated to testify in the prosecution of my employers are unable to testify, the case against them will be severely weakened, if not totally destroyed. Therefore, if I want to live to enjoy my retirement, those witnesses, namely you, must not be permitted to testify. If that sounds blunt, I suppose it is! But enough talk, I have never talked so much. It must be because I respect you. If you all will gather together on the other side of this table, I will do you the honor of making your deaths as painless as possible. Ethan, I see that you are beginning to get ideas again. Will you please join your wife?"

Henri motioned Ethan to Stephanie's side with the barrel of the automatic pistol, and as he did, Alex came up from behind him in a flying tackle. Alex had gone down to the helicopter to make sure the pilot came up to have something to eat, and was just coming back when he heard Henri. Henri half turned, since he had either seen or heard Alex's movement, and opened fire. Alex was hit seriously, but his momentum took him into Henri's legs and the sheer dead weight of Alex's body knocked 'Henri' off balance.

A sudden, sharp, imperative command from behind the grouped team and visitors was heard, "Hit the dirt!" That command was obeyed by almost everyone, even by the chancellor, and as 'Henri' regained his balance, three shots hit him, one in the head, and two dead-center. He was dead before he hit the ground. Leigh came up from her shooter's stance and holstered the still smoking automatic. Ethan, who had, as he did once before, managed to land on top of Stephanie and now rolled off to let her catch her breath.

"Where did you come from," asked the chancellor of Leigh, not that I'm complaining!"

"After I had my people all set for a review, for some reason, I thought that this whole scene would make a pretty target. Maybe it might be best if we weren't seen after all, so I had my people hide the trucks and themselves, as best they could, as quickly as they could! After lunch I went down to where they were assembled, to ready them for a review before our guests left. I guess that was a good idea!"

"Talk about people with good ideas! You saved us, Leigh, "Thank you!" remarked Stephanie.

It was Leigh's turn to redden, and in her best movie accent replied, "Aw, twern't nothing, Ma'am!"

Ethan had made his way to Alex, kneeled beside him, and choked back a sob.

A weak, but very much alive voice said, "I ain't dead yet, Mr. Ethan!"

Ethan yelled for the medics, and Alex was soon being tended and treated as the hero he was.

The chancellor realized he didn't have a pilot, so he called for one to fly down. This time he called the governor and asked for a National Guard pilot. Due to the recent circumstances, the governor was glad to oblige.

The chancellor and the two professors sat inside the big house. The adventures of the afternoon had sapped them, and they decided that the great outdoors of the western Central Valley was just a little too much for them.

Stephanie had started to say to no one in particular, that there was so much to do, but stopped herself before the words came out. She knew how lucky she was to be alive, to be loved by this man who had demonstrated his love for her again and again, and to have people who respected her, listened to her, and valued her ideas. Their lives had been saved by Leigh, who had come in a military capacity, but had also become a wonderful friend. She couldn't help marveling a bit about the events of the summer.

Once again, as the approaching evening breeze picked up a bit, it blew the built up tension of the day away. Ethan started the generator and the lights were lit, not for the security of the glowing illumination this time, but for the light in which to relax and to eat. The food was replenished and everyone began to realize, given the recent drama, how good it was to be alive. Stephanie moved a bit closer to Ethan on the porch swing, and Leigh lounged in a nearby lawn chair, and all sat quietly together. Alex, the other hero of the day, had been bundled up, supported by pillows, and sat peacefully in an overstuffed porch chair, a little wan, but softly whistling a nameless tune.

Members of the guard's musical group started up a lazy, western, evening tune. Soon, the members of the research team were drawn, as if mesmerized, from the one large and the many smaller tents to the well-tended grassy yard in front of the ranch house porch and started dancing to the music.

It wasn't long until the dancers were joined by those of the guard who were not on perimeter duty, drawn to the humming, softly flickering lights powered by the generator, as moths, to the lights of a flame. In the darkening shadow of the three hills in the background, the evening air was filled with the sounds of the humming electric generator, the buzzing lights, and the lilting notes of musical accompaniment emanating from an impromptu band, providing inspiration for a full-fledged dance under the lights in front of the ranch house. The lengthening shadow of the three hills were back lit by the last radiant rosy rays of the sinking sun behind them.

Printed in the United States
By Bookmasters